A SUITE LIFE

Other books by Sue Gibson:

A Suite Deal

A SUITE LIFE

•

Sue Gibson

AVALON BOOKS
NEW YORK

Published by Thomas Bouregy & Co., Inc.
160 Madison Avenue, New York, NY 10016

Library of Congress Cataloging-in-Publication Data
Gibson, Sue, 1957-
A suite life / Sue Gibson.
p. cm.
ISBN 978-0-8034-9922-5 (acid-free paper)   1. Women
painters—Fiction.   2. Hotelkeepers—Fiction   I. Title.
PR9199.4.G535S86 2008
813'.6—dc22

2008023801

PRINTED IN THE UNITED STATES OF AMERICA
ON ACID-FREE PAPER
BY HADDON CRAFTSMEN, BLOOMSBURG, PENNSYLVANIA

With great thanks to my remarkable family for accommodating both a writer's quirks and foibles and the inevitable inconveniences that arise while writing a book.
I promise, lunch at noon and dinner at five from now on—at least until the next book!

Chapter One

"**S**old!" Artie Townsend shoved the box of picture frames down on the table and angled his cane toward a tall wicker basket. He dragged it toward his chest and eyeballed the contents with an auctioneer's practiced eye, his stone-faced appraisal revealing nothing to the throng of onlookers.

With the tip of her finger, Delaney Forbes separated the strands of beads separating her hair-salon-slash-art-gallery from the storeroom, and watched the elderly auctioneer's arm disappear into the depths of the basket. She slapped her hand over her mouth before sliding it higher to cover her eyes. *Oh, no. I meant to throw those in the garbage.*

She inched forward on the wooden stool, mimicking

1

the crowd's en-masse shuffle toward the mysterious basket.

From the bottom of the basket the auctioneer hauled up two vinyl shoulder capes, both stained with hair dye and drops of peroxide. A collective sigh of disappointment rippled across the room.

Delaney dipped her head and felt the warm flush of embarrassment rush to her cheeks. What were they expecting? Ancient Egyptian tapestries? For heaven's sake, this is Buttermilk Falls, Ontario—population eight hundred and ten—not Cairo.

Delaney resettled on her perch and returned to picking at the seashell pink of her lacquered nails. *I should have just sold the artwork piecemeal,* she grumbled to herself. It would have been far less embarrassing.

No. She shook her head from side to side, slopping a trio of amber droplets from her Tim Hortons coffee cup to the right thigh of her new capri pants. No, an auction was the right choice. She closed her eyes and summoned up her mantra. *Think Paris, think Paris, think Paris.*

The City of Lights was calling, and this time she intended to obey her heart. In five short days she'd be on a plane destined for Paris, and heady freedom. So if that meant putting up with strangers rummaging through her stuff. . . . so be it.

Sweet liberation was so close she could almost smell it. She straightened her aching back and drew in a cleansing breath. An acrid aroma filled her nostrils and she reached to rub her nose. Apparently liberation smelled a lot like smoke.

The plaintive cry of a fire truck interrupted Artie's rapid-fire sales pitch. "Don't worry," Artie reassured his jittery audience, "probably just an overzealous barbecuer."

The crowd tittered appreciatively and Delaney concurred with Artie's verdict. After all, it was the height of cottage season on nearby Loon Lake.

She laced her fingers around her coffee cup. The warm liquid slid down her throat, and she wondered idly if Canada's favorite coffee outlet was franchised in Paris.

Her gaze skimmed the room. Thank goodness the rest of the items for sale were mostly reproductions of classics and a few framed pictographs—considerably less embarrassing stuff.

"Step right up, ladies and gents. Here's what you fine folks have all been waiting for."

The sea of heads swiveled at the auctioneer's gravelly demand.

Artie held up a reproduction of Monet's *Women in the Garden* framed in dark walnut. He propped it on an easel set next to his podium.

"Who will start me off?" Artie waved his cane over the crowd as if to hook them by their necks and draw them closer.

"Eighty dollars," a deep male voice boomed from the back.

Delaney twisted on her stool for a better look. Now

there's a face somebody should put on canvas, or at least on a bottle of aftershave.

The masculine voice belonged to Trey Sullivan. Athletic, thirtysomething, and a good head taller than the masses, with thick blond hair expertly razed by number three clippers and gelled to a perfect "George Clooney," straight from the pages of *Hairstyle Monthly*.

She reluctantly dragged her gaze from his chiseled face and refocused on the auctioneer and the next item. Thankfully just a box of frames. Her thoughts flew directly back to the hunky interim manager of the ritzy Nirvana hotel. What brought him to her small sale?

"Now, there's a man with a discerning eye," Artie called out. "Let's hear eighty-five. Eighty-five? Eighty-five anyone?"

Bids volleyed across the room and Delaney relaxed slightly. *Don't know why you're here, Ken-doll, but thank you very much for setting the tone. Paris, here I come.*

"Sold for one hundred and twenty dollars. Come collect your piece, sir."

The crowd shuffled apart, allowing the broad-shouldered man from the back to reach the auctioneer's podium. He smiled his thanks to the crowd, revealing a smile straight from a toothpaste commercial.

Delaney allowed the beaded curtain to slip from her fingers and smiled. She extracted a pen from behind her ear and with a flourish added the sale to her tally. It was starting to look like she might actually be able to start life in Paris with a clean slate.

Thank goodness the sexy Mr. Sullivan had shown up. And not just because the room was sadly lacking in eye candy. And if she felt a teensy bit awkward making a profit off Lily and Ethan's handsome best man, she glanced down to the rising total—she'd learn to live with it.

Thankfully, most folks in the room were Loon Lake cottagers, not her neighbors.

Over the past four years that she'd simultaneously run her art gallery and hairdressing salon (a girl needs to be resourceful in a small town), Buttermilk Falls' permanent residents had rarely purchased any artwork. They booked haircuts and perms and sat straight-backed in her funky black and chrome barber's chair while she trimmed or curled their hair. But the vibrant landscape paintings that she bought at estate sales and from local artists were purchased by the tourists that flooded the Region O' Rivers area of eastern Ontario each summer.

"Delaney?" Trey Sullivan's smooth baritone eased through the flimsy divider. "I was hoping I'd see you today."

His voice, deep and sexy like a late-night DJ, sent a spark sizzling down her spine. She sat up straighter on her perch. Both the compliment and the proximity of his body were disconcerting.

"Oh, really?" she blurted out, not really intending to sound rude. But seriously, she doubted he'd given her a second thought after their brief introduction at his boss's wedding reception. He'd been far too busy with his Barbie doll date to have taken more than a passing notice of her.

"What brings you into the village?" she said in a friendlier tone. "Slow day at the Nirvana?" If nothing else, twenty-seven years of living in Buttermilk Falls had taught her the fine art of small talk.

With her free hand she tucked a strand of hair behind her ear before centering her coffee cup strategically over the coffee spots decorating her thigh.

The fresh citrus smell of his upscale toiletries cut through the mustiness of the storeroom like a knife through butter as his shoulder further bulldozed the beaded curtain aside. She shot him a look she assumed was universal in interpretation. *Hello. Private Area.*

Obviously it meant nothing in his world.

His eyes crinkled at the corners as his gaze roved her face.

"You look every bit as gorgeous as you did the day of Ethan and Lily's wedding."

"Thanks." She shifted on the stool, raised the coffee cup to her lips, and tipped it high. Not even a drop.

She peeked over the rim and faked a swallow. Even after a lifetime of men complimenting her, she was still uncomfortable with overt male reaction.

Trey held his gaze. She squirmed a bit on the stool, but held her composure. *Man, but he is good-looking.*

Eventually his eyes dropped from her face to the paintings leaning against wall next to her chair. His hand settled on the dusty stack, and he split the pile open with his fingers. An abstract landscape done in primary colors blazed through the veil of dust particles. He bent eagerly to the signature at the bottom. "Now this is more like it!"

"No. Please don't." Heat rushed to her face and she snapped closed the gap. She'd painted them years ago while still in art school and had stored them in the humidity-controlled environment of the studio rather than in her home. There was no way Ken-doll was going to get a look at her work. Judge it. Find it lacking. Or worse, toss out throwaway compliments, all the while thinking her a hack.

She slid from the stool and, like a mother bear protecting her cubs from danger, inserted her body between his and the canvases. "Don't touch those! Only the pieces out front are for sale. *This* area is private." She flung her arm up and back, indicating the tiny space in which they stood.

He stepped back and raised his hands, flat-palmed, above his shoulders. "Okay. Calm down. I take it they're your work? Sorry."

Delaney waited for the pounding in her chest to slow before answering. "Er . . . yes, they're mine."

She resettled on the stool, crossed her legs, and folded her arms vise-like across her chest. A glance to his face confirmed he wasn't likely to push the issue any further.

If possible he looked even better chastised. Had she been too hard on him? Probably. But nobody got a crack at critiquing her paintings anymore. At least not until after Paris.

Suddenly she wished he'd go back to the sale. And take his good looks, good smells, and gobs of money with him. The very things that had other women falling at his Gucci-clad feet had the little voice in her head screaming foul. Nobody worth knowing could possibly be that perfect.

"Er . . . some excellent stuff is coming up, Trey. You might want to check it out." She nodded her head toward a heavyset man who was working his way closer to Artie's podium. "I bet that guy is after the Renoir copies."

"You bought some credible copies, Delaney, but I'm not looking for Renoirs. I've got twelve suites in the Nirvana's penthouse—all with bare walls—but I'm going in another direction. New artists. Maybe local artists." His glance flickered toward the forbidden paintings before turning back toward the gallery.

She ignored his none-too-subtle reference and leaned forward. He really did smell great. "Really? Well, you've come to the right community. This area of Ontario has become a real mecca for cutting-edge artists. In fact, many of them work at a communal studio not far from here." Her pulse quickened. How great it would be to see her friends' creations get the exposure they deserved.

His eyes remained on her face, so she kept talking.

"Do you have a central theme, or would every suite be different?"

"Undecided and open to suggestion." He turned, his brilliant smile back in place. "After all, a manager's job is mostly about communication, or at least that's what they taught me back in university."

"Do hotel managers generally choose the artwork?" Delaney knew her voice sounded incredulous, but she was floored. Since when did guys with MBAs know anything about art?

"Normally, no. Weatherall has a design team that looks after that. But the new Nirvana chain is Ethan's baby, so I'm doing him a favor on this one. Art is kind of a hobby of mine, and I've taken a few courses. And since he's still off honeymooning with the lovely Lily, and needs the final touches to the penthouse finished by the time he gets back, the job fell to me."

Delaney couldn't help but be a smidgen impressed. If Ethan Weatherall trusted Ken-doll with decorating his flagship hotel, then there had to be more to this guy than just a handsome face.

"So, why not hit the big auctions and galleries in the city?"

He grabbed the matching stool and settled in directly across from her. "I want to capture the flavor of this place. Find a look no other hotel would dream of trying. Every room different. Something to make our guests stop for a minute and. . . . think." He paused, sliced an opening in the beaded curtain with his tanned hand, and checked out the latest painting Artie was auctioning before adding, "And besides, Lily told me to come."

His face animated, he talked on, but she'd stopped listening. *How unfair is this? Pretty boy takes a few art classes and gets to showcase his vision of good art to half the world. I devote four long years to the Fine Arts program at the University of Toronto and end up dyeing the local senior set's hair varying hues of blue and hawking hotel art to the masses.*

She dragged her attention back to the moment. "And the Monet knockoff? How's that fit in with your plan?" A wonderful painting, she knew, but not exactly a startling departure from the norm.

"I'm staying in a penthouse suite and I'm tired of staring at blank walls. I'm here for the month, so I decided, where better to pick up something than here." His eyes crinkled at the corners, and he smiled his drop-dead-gorgeous smile in her direction. Brad Pitt had nothing on this guy.

Laughter bubbled up in her throat. You had to give him credit. His outrageous double entendre and engaging grin were a breath of fresh air.

Doing time in Buttermilk Falls for a whole month had to be killing him. No nightlife, unless he was planning on importing his crowd from the city, and most certainly no Barbie dolls.

Emboldened by her imminent departure from Buttermilk Falls, she played along. "That's gotta be a drag. Stuck in a hotel suite for weeks at a time."

"Oh, don't feel too sorry for me. Everything I need is just a phone call or elevator ride away. Room service. In-house gym. Spa. Gourmet dining." He threw up his hands and smiled. "Who needs a house."

"Well, I suppose a house would be a bit much for a single man." Lily had told her he was the quintessential bachelor. "You probably live in Toronto's downtown. A condo?"

"Seriously, Delaney, I live where I work. Suite 101 this week."

"Really?" She'd never met anyone without an address.

"I've got the perfect job. Ethan Weatherall's go-to guy. I go to India, Paris, Mexico—wherever there's a Weatherall Hotel and a problem. I stayed in the London penthouse all last week." A smile narrowed his bird's egg-blue eyes. "Don't need or want a picket fence."

Her own dandelion-infested backyard flashed through her mind, complete with her neighbor and Buttermilk Falls' lone real estate agent, Flo Reading, peering over their shared cedar hedge, giving tips on how to land a husband. *Argh.*

Right in front of her stood a real-life Nowhere Man. With no laundry, no yard work, no pets, no nosy neighbors. Each new day full of possibility and total indulgence.

Her gaze traveled from his designer loafers to his lightly tanned face. Respect replaced annoyance. Here was a man who freely admitted that the status quo didn't interest him in the least.

She smiled, and through her lashes glanced up to his face. "I'm fascinated. Tell me more."

Trey watched Delaney Forbes' demeanor change from barely concealed tolerance to admiration. *Wow.* Usually when women learned of his globe-trotting ways and dedicated avoidance of domestic bliss, they'd immediately try to convince him otherwise. They'd smile Mona Lisa smiles and twitter, "Oh, but you don't know what you're missing."

His gaze returned to the couples in the showroom. Oh, he definitely knew what he was missing: routine, a scheduled existence, noisy kids and smelly pets, consulting a mate about, well, everything. He'd stood strong as his single counterparts fell out of contention for powerful jobs when they'd succumbed to the charms of a beautiful woman who dreamed of kids and a house in suburbia.

He turned to face the attractive woman who had the power to shorten his month-long sentence in Buttermilk Falls. She's just what he needed to speed up the entire project. "Too bad you're off to Paris. You're just the woman I need."

Her green eyes flashed in amusement. "Lonely already? Sorry to disappoint you, Trey, but I'm sure you'll find someone else to keep you company until Ethan dispatches you to a more exciting locale. How long have you been here, a week?" She shot him a bright but completely dismissive smile.

He rolled his eyes upward. Now this was awkward. Yes, she was gorgeous, but he wasn't looking for a local *entanglement*—just some expert artistic advice. "Uh, I meant, I need someone with significant expertise to help me find local artwork. I've full authority to hire staff. Er. . . . not that you're not completely attractive. . . ."

Spots of pink lit her cheekbones as he scrambled for the words that would put them back on even footing. Up until he'd stuck his foot in his mouth, he hadn't had this much fun since he'd landed in this dot-on-the-map.

"Didn't Lily mention that I'm moving to France for a year?" she cut in. "In fact, I leave in five days." She raised her hand, like a crossing guard warning school kids to stop and obey. "I'm sure you'll find someone else to help you out."

"Just hear me out, Delaney. I need an assistant for one short month. Someone who knows the local artisans. Someone with courage to think outside the box. Come on, think about it. Paris isn't going anywhere." *What possible difference could it make*, he wondered, *when she left for her artsy sabbatical?*

"Keep looking, Trey. As tempting as it sounds, I can't take the job," she said in a louder voice. "I'm leaving Buttermilk Falls." Annoyance darkening her pretty features, she stared defiantly into his face.

Who was she trying to convince—me or herself? he wondered as the auctioneer smacked his gavel, announcing another sale. His gaze fell to the cluttered table beside her stool. On a sheet of yellow lined paper, a tidy row of figures stretching down the right-hand side listed today's sales. According to the calculations, she'd accumulated nine hundred and twelve dollars.

"Four thousand dollars and an expense account," he said, mentally discarding the lesser sum he'd planned on offering.

"What?" Her shiny black hair swooped across her cheek and grazed her narrow shoulder as her head tipped to one side. Confusion creased her forehead and pursed her lips. Curvy, soft lips.

"That's your salary for four weeks. It's what I'd pay for the service in the city." Sure they would also have an established office complete with pandering assistants and all the right connections. But a bold move was required here. "And if you're as good as Lily says, then you're worth every cent."

He could almost see the calculations going on behind eyes as dark as espresso coffee. Paris would be a lot more fun with a pocketful of cash, he knew. He rocked back on his heels and consulted his watch, allowing her a moment to compose a dignified acceptance.

"Again, Mr. Sullivan, no. Thank you." Her voice was softer now, as if she was explaining a difficult concept to a child. "Some things can be put off, but this trip isn't one of them. I *will* be in Paris in a couple of days, not Buttermilk Falls."

His stomach sank with her refusal. It would have been exciting to work side-by-side with Delaney Forbes. Although he could easily picture her in Paris with her shiny black hair held back with some flimsy scarf thing as she strolled along the Left Bank. And most likely, a guy named Pierre would be waiting for her at a little bistro.

She sounded completely determined to leave her childhood home. Understandable. Admirable even, he considered, glancing out the tiny rear window to a row of cluttered backyards crowded with swing sets and clotheslines. He totally got it.

He'd escaped his own suburban prison when he'd left for university. He loved his parents for providing him a stable childhood, but he'd intentionally carved out a bigger life for himself.

His eyes went back to Buttermilk Falls' most cosmopolitan and delicious citizen, as he gloomily anticipated his next four weeks of hard time in Hicksville.

She pointedly examined her empty paper cup and hopped from her perch. "I'm off. Time for another cup of coffee," she announced as she exited through the back door. "Enjoy the rest of the auction."

Yes, the completely charming Delaney Forbes belonged in Paris, he allowed, as he shouldered back through the flimsy beaded curtain. But why did it have to be on his time?

Chapter Two

The trip to Tim Hortons doughnut shop was anything but routine. She'd met the police chief, Sergeant Wilson, just as she entered the shop, and he'd immediately pulled her aside to relay the shocking news. Aborting her coffee run, she'd raced back to the auction.

The gallery's door slammed behind her, propelling the wind chimes into a clacking frenzy. She charged back into the room she'd vacated only ten minutes earlier and scanned for a woman dressed in floral polyester.

There she was, front and center, her bountiful chest still heaving. "Flo Reading, exactly what happened?" Delaney demanded and braced for a convoluted tale rife with unrelated details.

"Delaney, I'm so sorry!" Flo wailed as she strained to rise from the depths of the giant barber's chair where she'd collapsed moments earlier. "But don't worry, the fire in your kitchen is out," she announced to Delaney and curious onlookers alike. Flo wiped pearls of sweat from her upper lip with a flowered sleeve and accepted Artie's help in resettling her trembling body in the chair.

"Flo, calm down," Artie cautioned, "it's not worth having an episode over." He patted her shoulder and smiled at his audience through clenched teeth, dipping his head and whispering in Flo's ear, "The auction is almost over, just rest a bit until I finish up."

He pointed the hook end of his cane toward his nervous audience. "Come on back," he called out. "Nothin' at all to concern yourselves with."

Mollified, eighty-plus eyes refocused on the next item up for bid.

Delaney pressed her fingertips to her temples. *All I wanted was a second cup of coffee and suddenly my whole world blows up.* Minutes earlier, when she'd slipped over to Timmy's, Sergeant Wilson had informed her of the blaze at 31 Lilac Lane, the house her parents had vacated four years ago when they'd moved to Calgary to be closer to Delaney's brother and their three grandchildren; the house that was subsidizing her much anticipated year in Paris.

"No use going home to check damage just yet," the police chief had said, cutting into the line for a refill. "The volunteer firefighters have the scene taped off. Talk to Flo," he'd advised, and nodded down the street toward Delaney's storefront. "She ran out of your place hell-bent on breaking the upsetting news herself." As Delaney turned to leave, he'd placed a hand as big as a bear paw on her forearm and said, "Rest assured I gave those boys a real talking-to and told them to show up at the fire station to help clean equipment every Saturday for a month."

Sergeant Wilson stood well over six feet tall, with Hulk Hogan arms and size thirteen feet—an intimidating figure even to most adults. So by virtue of the police officer's stature alone, Delaney had the satisfaction of knowing the boys hadn't escaped unpunished.

Hands on hips, Delaney fixed her gaze on Flo. She should have known better than to have signed on with Flo's real estate company in the first place. Calamity accompanied Flo in most of her endeavors. A trait her twin boys had inherited in spades. It wasn't the first time Sergeant Wilson had to deal with the Reading boys, but hopefully the last.

Flo's gaze deserted Delaney's and sought out a woman in the crowd with two young children in tow and smiled in a conspiratorial manner before beginning with, "Boys will be boys, you know."

Delaney felt her jaw tighten. Flo's boys? More like little demons in matching Gap outfits.

"Completely by accident, they set a teeny little fire in your kitchen while I was showing your house to the Johnson family.

You know, ever since Sid ran off with that floozy from

Tay Valley, I've pretty much had to take the kids with me everywhere. I left the boys playing in your kitchen while I showed your house again to the Johnsons—you know, the young couple I found who plan on renting it while you're overseas. They'd called earlier and asked if they could come in and measure for curtains. They absolutely hate blinds of any kind and had found some material on sale—"

"Flo, the fire." Tears born of fear and frustration welled behind Delaney's eyes, and she blinked rapidly. "Is everything burnt?"

"Oh, no. Nothing like that. Apparently, Teddy and Freddy lit—just for fun, you know—a wee fire in a metal wastebasket. You see, last night at the Pioneer Club, all the children received flint stones. The whole troupe is going camping over on Osprey Island this weekend and you know my boys," Flo beamed proudly and drew a breath, "they so wanted to impress the leader with their fire-making skills."

"So, it's minor then. The damage is confined to the wastebasket?" Delaney said, biting back a nasty come-back relating to the deviant behavior of her neighbor's young sons. Flo had a blind spot the size of Montreal when it came to her twin boys.

"Well, there is a bit of smoke damage, but don't worry," she said, "I know a company over in Tay Valley that specializes in sanitizing fire sites. And when I got my real estate license I took out insurance to cover. . . . problems like this." She wrinkled her long, narrow nose and leaned in closer to whisper, "They'll steam that nasty smell right out of your walls and furniture. Your home will be as good as new when they're done. No one will ever know."

Delaney raised her eyes and without moving her head, allowed her gaze to rove the crowded room, "I think that ship has sailed, Flo."

"Just wait until you hear the good news, Delaney. The Johnsons have agreed to honor the lease—after I assured them the house would be in move-in condition soon. They said they didn't mind waiting the two extra weeks."

"Two weeks!" Delaney's hands clenched into fists and she stepped closer to Flo's glowing face. "I'm moving into a ridiculously overpriced studio apartment in Paris in four days. If I don't show up, the woman I'm sharing it with will rent my half of the room to someone else—in a heartbeat. It's the Rue de Vaugirard for heaven's sake." Now she was nose-to-nose with Flo. "I need that rent deposit now, not in two weeks."

"Oh, that's just not possible, dear," Flo said matter-of-factly. "They won't pay until the cleanup is finished."

Delaney felt a weight settle on her left shoulder and a warm breath sweep across the nape of her neck. "Maybe I can help?"

Why was he still here? Delaney whirled to face Trey. "Unless you've got a steam machine in the backseat of your Porsche, I doubt that very much."

"Sorry, no. But I do have a whole floor of empty

suites at the Nirvana, if that helps at all." Trey's sympathetic smile only served to further infuriate her.

Didn't anybody get it? She'd been so close to freedom. Her passport was in her purse. Three weeks ago she'd sold her hairdressing supplies and client list to Flo's cousin, Anna. That money disappeared with the purchase of a new high-efficiency furnace and a red steel roof for 31 Lilac Lane. She couldn't expect anyone to rent her house without making some long-overdue updates. The money from the art auction was earmarked to pay off her credit cards. She intended to leave for Paris with a clean slate.

She no longer had a job in this town and, thanks to Flo's little firebugs, no place to live. The last thing she could afford was an extended stay at the luxurious Nirvana Hotel.

"Nonsense, Delaney. What are neighbors for? You'll stay with me. I've loads of room," Flo interjected, shooting Trey a look laden with skepticism. "I'll just move my sewing machine and the boys' hockey equipment out of the spare room. No need at all to compromise your reputation."

The room swirled and Delaney reached for the back of the barber's chair and stared sightlessly at the tiled floor. *Where's Lily when I need her the most? Off honeymooning with her handsome husband,* Delaney thought, momentarily mired in self-pity. As if those short e-mails that popped up in her in-box every few days could replace their long talks over coffee and Timbits.

"It's settled then," Flo said, obviously taking Delaney's silence for agreement. "I'll go ahead home and you come along when you're ready. Oooh, it'll be fun, Delaney. Like a two-week slumber party."

The wind chimes tinkled and the suffocating scent of jasmine faded and Delaney knew Flo was gone. Delaney straightened and turned to face the crowd. Somehow the whole room had suddenly emptied out.

"I'll tally up and give you a call over at Flo's later," Artie called out and hurried out to the sidewalk to collect his sandwich-board signs.

She waved weakly to his departing back and turned to survey the bare walls. Trey's tall frame, silhouetted by the sun, loomed large against the creamy colored walls. She jumped and pressed her open palm over her racing heart. "You nearly scared me to death."

"Sorry. I didn't want to go without making myself clear." He stepped closer and smiled. "I wasn't trying to drum up business or suggest anything er. . . . inappropriate when I suggested you stay at the Nirvana."

"Oh." She wished he would just leave her alone, but he actually did sound sincere. Plus, she didn't want to be rude to Lily and Ethan's friend.

"Look, if Lily and Ethan were around, you know they'd offer you a free room at the Nirvana, right?"

"Well, I suppose they might."

"And I've already made you a legitimate job offer—which included a free suite," he reminded her. "It's not Paris, but the Nirvana's got a killer hot tub."

Delaney was torn.

She had no doubt that two weeks with Flo and the twins would be a nightmare of epic proportions. But on the other hand, she'd be right next door to her own house. Daily proximity and diligent supervision might motivate the cleanup crew to finish the job faster. And as much as she hated to admit it, living over at the Nirvana would send the gossip mill into overdrive. Her mother's friends had taken on a proprietary, maternal role ever since her parents had left town. In fact, one of them could be dialing her parents at that very moment, denying her the opportunity to break the upsetting news herself.

But on the other hand, she was twenty-seven years old. An adult. Her eyes locked with Trey's baby blues. His twofold offer had its own merit: private, posh accommodation and a dream job with a hefty income. Downside: his irresistible smile and boyish charm. A girl could get sidetracked, lose her focus. Maybe be persuaded to put Paris on hold for longer than it took to clean up her house.

"Thank you, Trey. But no," Delaney said. "I'm betting on the sanitation crew. If things go my way, I'll be sipping café au lait in a little Parisian café in less than two weeks." Her optimistic tone sounded forced even to her own ears, but she'd come too far to let her dream slip away now.

"Hey, you can't blame a guy for trying," he said, his tone not as light as the cliché demanded. He pulled his card from his shirt pocket. "Take this. In case you change your mind."

Halfway to the door he turned and flashed a smile. "You know, we have a lot in common, Delaney. I bet you love fine food." She bobbed her head in response. "How about dinner on the hotel's Trillium Terrace later this week? Just dinner, I promise."

Delaney sighed. Ken-doll obviously wasn't used to rejection from the ladies. She took another look and sighed again. He was like a long, cold drink to a woman living in a drought of datable men. And actually they did have some things in common. What harm could one little date possibly do?

Chapter Three

"Delaney, do you wanna play hide-and-seek again?" Freddy said, torpedoing his body across her narrow cot and cracking into the wall. "I promise not to forget to look for you this time."

"Sorry, Freddy, I told you once already about my date tonight. I need to get ready now." She looked pointedly toward the door and silently began to count to ten. *Give me patience*, she pleaded to the heavens. His brother had asked the same question five minutes ago while dribbling grape juice on the suede jacket she'd placed so carefully out on the bed.

"Can we come with you? Mom won't take us to real restaurants. Only the kind where you gotta stay in the car when you eat."

"No can do," she said, whirling to face the tallest of

the six-year-old twins. "It's a grown-up kind of place. Boring. You'd hate it." And so would the Nirvana's un-suspecting guests. She averted her eyes from a crest-fallen face sprinkled with freckles, complete with a missing front tooth and wondered how full-time par-ents ever managed to escape on their own.

She checked her look in the mirror. The loose-cut silky pants and matching sleeveless top would do just fine for a dinner on the Nirvana's terrace. Freddy's hamster had peed on her first choice, a cute little halter sundress.

Soon the machine gun din coming from the boys' room assured her they were now engrossed in a video game, and she turned to touch up her lipstick.

Was that the phone? She found herself holding her breath as she listened for a second ring. *Oh please, don't be Trey canceling our date.* With no job to go to, she'd been trapped in Flo's crazy household for five long days.

Ever since she'd dragged her aching body from the lumpy cot this morning, she'd been fantasizing about sipping Brazilian coffee on the Trillium Terrance with Loon Lake lapping against the rocky shore. The setting sun would warm the air and lend a flattering hue to her skin as she and Trey shared sophisticated banter. And there would not be one single dollop of Cheez Whiz gracing her plate.

"It's for you, Delaney," Teddy yelled, and tossed the cordless phone in the general direction of her bed be-fore racing back to his game. "It's Mommy."

Delaney extracted the sticky receiver from the waste

bin and spoke briskly into the phone while she headed for the stairs. She padded downstairs to the kitchen. "Flo. What's up?"

"Now, I know tonight is your big night out. Don't worry, I wouldn't dream of asking you to look after the boys a minute longer than necessary," Flo said. "I'll be home in a jiffy." Flo's real estate business kept her out most evenings.

So why was she calling, Delaney wondered, detecting a nervous quiver in Flo's voice.

"Have you been watching the news on television, Delaney?"

"No, you know the twins guard that remote like a couple of miniature Brinks security guards. We watched three hours of robot things smashing other robots to bits."

"There was an explosion in the boiler room over at Tay Valley Hospital. Apparently smoke billowed out through all the vents."

The sound of her own heartbeat filled her ears, and Delaney sunk into one the chrome chairs circling the kitchen table. She knew Marjorie from 3rd Street had been admitted yesterday with gallbladder trouble, and Herb from the post office was in for his angina again.

"Nobody hurt, thank goodness. The fire department evacuated the patients to the nursing home for the time being."

Delaney's pattering heart slowed to its normal rate. It could have been so much worse. Pride in the local volunteer firefighters welled in her heart. Before retiring to

Calgary, her father had often jumped from the dinner table when the fire bells pealed, leaving them to wonder and worry.

"Thanks for letting me know," Delaney said, snatching a box of Flo's hair dye from Teddy's grasp. "I'll check with the hospital tomorrow and see if there's anything I can do to help." At last, a valid reason to spend a day away from 33 Lilac Lane.

"Your mother brought you up right, dear friend," Flo said, her voice quaking. "And you're so good to my little angels."

A pang of guilt reddened Delaney's face as she remembered how frequently she'd wanted to throttle the twins this week.

"Anyway, I'll just make a quick call to the cleanup crew over at your house, and then I'll be right home. Toodles."

"Perfect." Delaney clicked the phone off and walked to the curtained window facing her small clapboard house.

Through the haze of Irish lace, the branches of an old maple tree cast its shadow in long, purplish fingers that stretched across the side yard like spilled grape juice. A clump of overgrown lilacs, its mauve blooms hanging heavy from an early afternoon sun shower, caught and held the sun in sparkling droplets.

Delaney dropped her head to the side and considered the possibilities. A small canvas for sure, with the house muted, almost blurry, and let the ancient maple tell the story. It was here first after all. Her fingers twitched at her sides and she acknowledged the need. Soon, she reminded herself, soon. She'd given up painting four years ago to pursue a more practical and less ego-damaging career, but the decision had never been fully sanctioned by her heart.

Parting the lace curtains with a finger, she watched workmen, in white one-piece overalls, trek back and forth from the side door to a huge work truck. Like a well-oiled machine they loaded vacuum hoses, pails, and crates.

Delaney narrowed her eyes to better focus and sucked in a breath. They'd never loaded up their equipment at the end of the day before. She pressed her nose closer to the glass. Yes, they were definitely clearing everything out. Were they finished?

Relieved that her move to Paris was apparently back on track, she spun to face the twins and called out, "One more round of hide-and-seek, anyone?" The thrill of impending escape unfurled the knot that had formed in her stomach the day of the auction. "You've got two minutes and then I'll start looking." Gosh, they really were kind of cute when they smiled.

Thirty minutes later and her second outfit languishing in the laundry hamper, Delaney paced the floor, purse in hand. She checked the driveway again and smoothed her hair behind one ear. Where was Flo? It was amazing how often last-minute errands held up Flo's return to the twins.

If Flo didn't arrive before Trey, she'd have to invite him into the house. She glanced around the living room. Heaps of toys cluttered a room dominated by a blaring big-screen TV. The boys, now with dishtowels knotted around their waists, took shots at one another with well-placed karate kicks.

Just as she was reaching for the phone to ask Trey to delay their dinner reservation, it jangled for the second time. Yanking back her hand, she glared at the offending machine. What news would Flo announce this time?

Delaney stiffened her backbone and steeled herself against what would be a laundry list of excuses from the twins' absent mother. *Be calm, but firm,* she reminded herself. *Flo is a businesswoman. She'll respect my insistence that she come right home.*

"Hello," she said, digging deep for a strong and assertive tone.

The line buzzed for a second. "Ummm. Delaney?"

The male voice on the other end was deep and sexy.

"Oh, Trey, it's you," she said, reverting to her normal voice. "I thought it might be Flo." Wow. Was it possible to sound handsome? "I'm ready, but Flo's not home yet, so I'm still babysitting the twins."

She glanced to the messy room and shrugged her shoulders. "But you may as well head over, so we can leave as soon as Flo arrives."

"I'm flattered. You obviously can't wait to see me," he said.

She tucked her tiny clutch purse under one arm and smiled into the phone. "You, and a menu. I don't know what time you usually eat, but I'm starving."

"Is that all I am to you, a meal ticket? You're killing me," he said, picking up on her frivolous mood.

"Of course not. You're taking me dancing in the Starlight Room afterward too!"

Trey laughed out loud. "Apparently, I am."

"Hey, I'm leaving town next week. It might be my last chance to check out Buttermilk Falls' newest and only hot spot."

His voice became more subdued, "Still determined to leave all of Buttermilk Falls' single guys high and dry as of next week."

"Plane ticket number two is already in my purse. And as for the local eligible bachelors—I've dated all four of them at some point in the past. Trust me, no matches made in heaven are about to be lost." The problem was that most single men her age were looking to settle down, raise some kids, and didn't understand her restlessness. Somehow she knew the uneasiness would remain until she knew for certain whether she was meant to paint again. Paris held all the answers.

Trey chuckled into the phone. "Well, I can't speak for the others, but over here at the Nirvana, number five is feeling kind of blue."

She found herself smiling. It was fun to talk with someone who got her. She still confided in Lily, of course, but lately Lily was insanely preoccupied with her husband and the new home she and Ethan planned to build on Loon Lake when they returned.

"That's just your hunger talking. And hey, you're not

a local. A big-city guy like you has thousands of single gals to choose from."

"All right, you've got me there."

A smidgen of disappointment at his quick agreement diminished her upbeat mood slightly.

"Anyway," he went on, "the reason I called is to find out what you feel like eating. I usually preorder with the chef. What do you say? Lobster, steak, chicken?"

Her mouth filled with saliva. Almost every night this week she'd faced down a plate of microwaved hot dogs with a side helping of gooey macaroni and cheese. "Oh, lobster, please." She hopped up and down like a five-year-old waiting for a piece of cake at a birthday party.

"I picked lobster too. Why settle for anything but the best, right?"

"Exactly."

"I'll be right over. Third house on Lilac Lane, right?"

"Ye. . . . ss. The pink and white house with the plastic flamingos in the flower bed," she confirmed before he said good-bye and clicked off.

Delaney returned to her post by the window, the smudged glass reflecting her upturned lips. Obviously, Trey had taken the time to track her whereabouts this week. She pictured him cruising in his Porsche, searching for the street named after its abundant lilac bushes.

Her smile broadened. She was determined to remain unattached, but she wasn't dead.

Chapter Four

"No," Delaney said flat out, "that's impossible."

Flo hung her coat in the hallway closet and turned to face Delaney's shocked face. "It's out of my hands, hon. Those poor patients evicted from the hospital need the services of the cleaning crew right now. Beds are lining the halls of the nursing home!" Flo dusted her hands together and headed toward the kitchen.

Was Flo serious? Had Buttermilk Falls' only smoke-damage company pulled out of her house? Instantly, she felt bad. Of course they had.

Delaney called out to Flo in the kitchen. "Have you told the Johnsons this new bit of information yet?" Apprehension tightened her chest. If her tenants couldn't wait a month and found another house to rent, then all her plans were up in smoke too. She needed their rental income to pay her for her studio apartment in Paris.

"That's why I'm late." Flo turned and flashed a smile over her shoulder before announcing proudly, "It took some doing, but they said they loved your little place so much, they're willing to wait it out."

"Thanks for handling that, Flo," Delaney began, "I can't possibly stay with—"

"Of course you can. Don't you worry about staying with me and my boys. You're hardly any trouble at all."

"That's not what I meant. . . ."

Delaney flattened her body against the wall as Flo maneuvered past with a box of crackers in one hand and a jar of peanut butter held high over her head in the other.

"By the way," Flo said over her shoulder, "I forgot to tell you that tomorrow night is my turn to host the twins' Pioneer Club. If you could just cover for me for a bit—you know, make some snacks and entertain the troupe until I get here. . . ."

Delaney slid slowly to the carpet, her back displacing a jumble of hockey sticks. The clattering collapse went unheeded by the living room trio. They were either immune to all the noise, or deaf from years of living in it.

Delaney shoved aside the sticks with her elbow and contemplated her situation. An artist needs peace and solitude to paint. Her muse required a garret flat on the rue d'Anjou. And Delaney needed the Johnsons' rent checks in hand when she boarded the plane.

"Delaney, come squeeze in here on the couch," Flo mumbled through a mouthful of peanut butter and crackers, "*WrestleMania* starts in two minutes."

Delaney cringed and drew her legs up to a fetal position. "No, thanks. Trey should be here any second," she called out.

"Oooh, Trey. I love you," erupted from the twins, followed by fake kissing.

Delaney pressed her fingers to her temples and rotated them gently. *I'll go crazy if I stay in this house for another month.*

From the driveway she heard the crunching of gravel announcing the arrival of Trey's Porsche. She scrambled to her feet and dusted off her black, majorly discounted Alfred Sung pants. Smoothing her silky black halter top into place, she drew in a breath and composed her face. Her white knight awaited.

She swung the door open and faced an empty space. No tall, dark, handsome man with a brilliant smile, cradling flowers in the crook of his arm stood on the other side. She glanced to the empty Porsche idling in the driveway.

"Delaney, please give me a month. I know you said no before. But I need your help, big-time," Trey pleaded from a place just below and to the right of her kneecap. "I tried tracking down the local artists myself. I need your help. And where the heck is Black Creek Road anyway? I drove around the lake for at least two hours and came home empty-handed."

She looked down into his head of thick, sandy-brown hair. In what fairy tale did white knights beg for help from stressed-out damsels? "Get off your knees," she whispered, "the whole neighborhood is watching. By tomorrow afternoon the Bluebird's brunch crowd will have gossiped your little charade into a full-blown marriage proposal."

"If that's what it takes to get you to work with me, then—" Trey grabbed her clenched fist and planted a loud kiss, reminiscent of Teddy and Freddy's earlier version, on the back of her hand.

She yanked her hand free. "Too late, buster. You already showed your cards, remember—at the auction. No picket fences in your future. A girl in every port or something. . . ."

Trey slammed his open palm into his forehead. "I talk way too much. And it was hotel, not port."

"I stand corrected."

"Well then, back to my first offer. How about it, Delaney? I'll throw in a company car for your use."

Delaney glanced across the lawn to her own driveway and her fourteen-year-old rusting Cavalier. She bit her bottom lip.

A loud crash followed by Teddy's high-pitched war cry pierced the lilac-scented evening air and returned her attention to the problem at hand. Could she last another four weeks in the same house as Flo and the twins? She turned to face Trey.

His profile, caught in light and shadow, revealed a

strong, angular jaw and a straight nose with a little bump near the bridge. A soft sigh slipped from her lips. Why couldn't a guy like this have shown up on her door-step years ago? It certainly would've made life in Buttermilk Falls a lot more interesting.

But really, was there no good reason not to let him play the White Knight for a month? Isn't that how he billed himself—the kind of hero that saves the day and then rides off into the sunset?

She definitely needed some help and his riding away at the end of the month coincided perfectly with her own agenda. "Is your offer of a free suite at the Nirvana still on the table?" She'd find a way to explain it to her mom later.

His movie star smile lit up the porch. "Absolutely."

Chapter Five

High above the Trillium Terrace, thousands of stars twinkled in the night's inky sky. As if held by an invisible string, an orange-slice moon dangled above the spruce trees. Buffered by the terrace's thick terra-cotta half wall, soft jazz tunes mixed with the buzz of mannerly, grown-up conversation.

Trey watched Delaney settle her dessert fork to her plate.

"I don't want to leave," she said.

"You don't have to," Trey replied. "The Trillium Terrace doesn't close until midnight."

Delaney's hand flew to cover her mouth. "Did I say that out loud? It's just so peaceful here." She ducked her head slightly, her feisty confidence looking all the more like girlish charm now.

"Don't be embarrassed. That's how you're supposed to feel, when you're in a Weatherall hotel," he said, pride surging in his chest. "We're famous for our romantic ambience."

He and Ethan had burned the midnight oil many nights developing this oasis. A place their clientele would revisit in real time, and in their memories.

"You don't have to sell me on the Nirvana, Trey. It's beautiful." She turned her head slowly, as if studying every chair and planter and tile, only stopping when her gaze met the drop-away view of Loon Lake. "I can't believe you live like this all the time. I'm jealous."

"What can I say, somebody's gotta do it. And as soon as you move in, it's your lifestyle too." He cocked his eyebrow toward Jason, the new busboy, and waited until he cleared the cutlery and plates before speaking. "It would be frozen dinners for me every night if I owned a home."

No need to mention that many evenings the chair across from him sat empty. The lifestyle had a downside too.

"Look, Trey," her voice softened, "I want to thank you for the job. I need the money and, quite frankly, I wasn't going to last another day at 33 Lilac Lane. I'm just not used to, you know"—she eyed the other diners as if checking for eavesdropping locals—"the family thing."

Her nose wrinkled prettily at the bridge with her whispered words. He couldn't imagine her living with

Flo and the gang either. Delaney Forbes fit perfectly with the Nirvana's cosmopolitan crowd. He glanced around the terrace, recognizing returning clientele from around the globe. Yes. She belonged in this world.

Too bad this world included Paris. For the third time this week he found himself wishing she didn't have one foot out of Buttermilk Falls. She could make his stay a lot more interesting.

Jason returned and placed a scented candle in the squat sandstone carving that served as a holder. "Mr. Sullivan," he whispered, "I thought you might like to know the band is warming up in the lounge."

"Thanks, Jason. Good job tonight."

Trey studied the college student as he moved about the tables. The young man's skills were top-notch, but it was his attitude that impressed him the most. Another name to add to Weatherall's list of potential interns.

"Shall we?" He cocked his head toward the strains of music drifting from the Starlight Room. "You said you expected dancing tonight. And I always try to please my date."

Delaney lifted her gaze to his face, steeling herself against the inevitable smug smile. She hated to insult her new boss, but *come on*, Trey, that line was beyond cheesy.

The dark eyes staring back at her revealed an intelligent mind. She held his gaze and let the moment stretch. His eyes crinkled at the corners and his smile seemed genuine, not smug. No veiled innuendo there, she decided with relief, just a confident statement. Well, maybe a bit overconfident, but not sleazy.

"Let's do it." She placed her hand in his open palm. "I love jazz."

The band played slow, smoky tunes. The kind that made you feel like you're falling in love as you slip-slide around the dance floor in the arms of your partner. And it's not until the band quickens the tempo and you peel yourself off your date that you realize it wasn't love, but the magic of a good jazz vocalist and a slow back beat that had you salivating against his shoulder.

Delaney loosened her arms slightly from around Trey's neck. It's the music. Definitely the music.

The five-piece band was incredible. The Starlight Room was incredible. And Trey? She sneaked a peek at her dance partner. He looked incredible.

Granted, coming off a week of babysitting the twin terrors, her judgment might be a tad skewed, but she was pretty sure she was dancing with the best-looking guy in the room.

"Who ever came up with the idea to let the real stars shine through was a brilliant designer," she commented, tipping her head to the glass expanse that substituted for a regular roof.

"Ethan worked with the architects on that one. He poured everything he had into this hotel. Had a lot riding on it and pulled out all the stops."

"I know. Lily told me that Ethan had to convince his

father that a high-end hotel in rural Ontario could pull in the business." She looked over his shoulder and around the room. It was crowded with young urban professionals enjoying a reprieve from their fast-paced city lives. "Obviously Ethan knew if he built the luxury hotel, the moneyed would come."

"I know it sounds corny, but Ethan had a dream, a passion. And he didn't rest until he accomplished it. The fact that he found Lily, the love of his life here at Loon Lake too, is amazing."

Delaney agreed wholeheartedly with Trey. *Big dreams aren't corny. Nor is a big, crazy love.* A stab of envy darted through her.

"I couldn't be happier for Lily and Ethan," she agreed, meaning it with all her heart.

Yes, her lifelong friend had found her own personal nirvana with the CEO of the Weatherall hotel chain. Ethan and Lily had fallen in love—not just any old love but a magnificent, black-and-white movie kind of love. So big that it had changed Delaney too, just by association.

Lily's marriage and defection from her best friend's everyday doings had forced Delaney to examine her own life.

She'd begun to wonder if it was time to face her fears and begin to paint again.

Paris was the answer, she'd decided. A fresh start. She'd devote a whole year to proving Noah Cravet, the *Toronto Daily*'s art columnist who had royally trashed her first major show, wrong. Four years ago, after her first show in Toronto, he'd called her uninspired, another wannabe who should hang up her brushes and find a day job. And that's exactly what she did.

But when she finally arrived in Paris, she intended to immerse herself in her art, mingle with other artists, and visit museums and galleries. And more importantly she'd finally pick up her paintbrushes again.

Somehow Lily's passion for Ethan had reignited Delaney's desire to harness the beauty that had been stifled inside her, blocked at her fingertips for too long. It was time to let it loose on a canvas. Share it with the world; make a career happen. Move to Paris!

And anyway, finding the right guy wasn't everything.

The sweet, musky fragrance of Trey's aftershave filled her nostrils. Man, he smelled delicious. Whoa. Back up. She better not become intoxicated by this man. As they circled by the open doors to the terrace, she sucked in a breath of fresh air.

Fortified, she relaxed in his arms. His chin grazed the front of her forehead, its angled edge rough against her skin.

Okay, that's it. Delaney pushed gently against his chest, stepped back, and turned toward the open French doors. "Let's take a break," she murmured.

The pressure of Trey's hand in the small of her back as he guided her through the sea of swaying bodies suddenly felt presumptuous and she quickened her step.

Trey lengthened his stride to keep pace with Delaney's

lanky legs. Her flimsy sandals clattered against the slate tiles as she sped across the patio toward the outer wall of the Trillium Terrace, and the view the hotel's brochure deemed spectacular.

He didn't know what caused the abrupt ending to their slow-dancing, but generally when a woman wanted to be alone in the dark under the stars it boded well for him to follow.

"Everything all right? You look a little flushed." Actually she looked gorgeous. Her cheeks were pink and glowing. The offshore breeze lifted strands of her shiny black hair and twirled them prettily around her face.

"Too warm. That's all. No other reason," she prattled, twisting her wrist to check her watch. "Oops. It's later than I realized."

"It's nine fifteen. That's early even in Buttermilk Falls." Was she ticked off about something?

"Are you kidding? Bet you ten dollars that when you drive me home, every living room light on Lilac Lane will be out."

Now that's the Delaney I know. Funny, outspoken, lighthearted. "You're on."

He reached to shake her slim left hand, hanging on to it a bit longer than sealing the deal required.

She shot him a wary look, extracted her hand, and crossed her arms over her chest. "Look, Trey. I think I should clear up something right now."

Her voice didn't sound lighthearted anymore. *What, did she have a mysterious boyfriend lurking in the bushes?* He didn't think so. Not according to the ladies at the Bluebird Café anyway.

His casual comment regarding Delaney's auction sale and an offer of a round of coffee had loosened the blue-haired gals' tongues to the point that he'd come away feeling he'd broken the rules of fair play.

Delaney hated gossip, he'd figured. It was probably one of the reasons she wanted to jump from her fishbowl into the big sea.

"Okay. Shoot. What do we need to talk about?" He stuffed his hands into his pockets and leaned against the terra-cotta wall.

She cleared her throat. "First, thanks again for the job. It's perfect for me, and I promise you won't regret giving me this opportunity."

He knew that already. "Go on."

"But this," she said, waving a finger back and forth between them, "you and I. . . ." Her face reddened and she cleared her throat again. "Look. I'll admit to an. . . . attraction." Her face colored again. "But I'm only here for the month. I intend to fly free and romantically unencumbered to Paris in four weeks. There's no room in my life for any. . . . er, relationship," she stated, placing air quotes around her final word.

"Oh." He'd heard this speech before—just not directed at him. He was the original author of the let's-keep-this-casual-and-fun-and-nobody-will-get-hurt speech.

He couldn't deny it stung a bit. But he admired her guts and honesty.

"No problem. And I'll admit to a certain attraction to you as well. We're in the same boat. Ethan hired me to get this job done and then, I'm out of here."

Her head bobbed in immediate agreement.

He scrambled for a way to keep her from exiting the relationship, or at least the Trillium Terrace. "We obviously enjoy each other's company," he said, his feet moving a step closer as if they had a mind of their own. "We enjoy the same things, art, good food, fine things." He held up his hands and hitched up his shoulders. "What's the problem?"

A small smile sweetened her lips. "Well, when you put it that way. I guess it would be fairly safe to. . . . since we both know it's a time-limited engagement.

"Your work at the Nirvana will be done in a month. I leave for Paris in a month. You love a job that takes you around the globe. I need to take my oils and brushes to Paris and immerse myself in my work, alone. I had a chance once before, and I let it get away from me."

Her voice dropped with her last statement. But when she lifted her head it was desperation flashing from her black eyes, not sadness. And the tears that threatened to fall were quickly blinked back.

He wanted to wrap his arms around her, pull her to his chest and say something helpful. But that would only send her running.

She was a strong woman, not willing to be sidetracked by a man or a job. He knew from their first meeting that Delaney Forbes was different. Not to mention fun, talented, and drop-dead gorgeous. Anyway, what man ever got roped and corralled in one short month? By the end of June, his job here was finished and he was, hopefully, off to Morocco.

"I think there is a way to have the best of both worlds. You and I can date. Keep it casual, fun," Trey said. "And I promise," he said while crossing his heart like a schoolboy, "never to get in the way of your painting-in-Paris dream."

Delaney flipped up her impossibly long eyelashes to expose the kind of eyes a man sinks into and doesn't care if he ever climbs out from again. "And I promise not to start building a white picket fence around your suite and ply you with home-cooked meals and hand-knit slippers."

"It's a deal." Instantly his stay in the boonies, which had seemed interminably long, shortened. Only four short weeks to hang with Delaney. He'd better get started. "Why don't we start off your new job tomorrow with a breakfast meeting? Can you be packed and ready by eight? I'll send a car over to Lilac Lane for you and your things."

Her broad smile spoke volumes. "I'll be ready and waiting, bags in hand."

Chapter Six

Delaney slipped up the stairs and padded into the spare room. It was just past 9:30 P.M., but as she'd predicted, Flo's house was dark and eerily quiet. She reached for her laptop and clicked until the friendly voice announced her unread e-mails. Eager to see if Lily had sent another message from Europe, Delaney inched closer to the flickering screen. There it was. Chock-full of interesting tidbits too.

Dear Delaney,

Yesterday, Ethan surprised me with a balloon ride over the Mediterranean Sea. The color of the water was indescribable, and I thought of you. Hope you get a chance to paint this someday. Glad you decided to accept Trey's job offer. Like Trey, Ethan and I are sure you'll do a great job. It's perfect for you. Have fun. Mrs. Lily Weatherall (doesn't that sound wonderful!)

The Nirvana's breakfast crowd had thinned out considerably since Trey had directed her to a small table nestled in the corner. Throughout breakfast his manner had been all business, no wisecracks, not one single sexy innuendo even. Delaney leaned back against her chair's upholstered back as the waiter cleared the plates and cutlery. She nodded her head enthusiastically to another refill of the restaurant's gourmet coffee, an adequate replacement for her Timmy's brew.

"So in a nutshell, Delaney, your job is to get a feel for the penthouse floor, present me with a written proposal outlining your vision and ideas, and then proceed to search out and acquire the artwork. Your time frame is a month, and I'll provide you with a generous purchasing budget."

Delaney felt the blood course through her veins. She was hungry to see the rooms, excited by the job that lay ahead of her. "I can't wait to get started, Trey."

"Super. But first I'll take you to your room and you can get settled in. I had the porter deliver your luggage already."

For the first time since he'd greeted her at the front desk, he smiled his familiar cat-and-mouse smile. "I take it you weren't kidding about being anxious to move out of Flo's. The driver said you were sitting on your suitcase at the end of the driveway."

"Yes, I'm excited about my new job," she replied, ignoring his attempt to turn the conversation more personal. In fact, she'd already called Alison Kaye, a potter who belonged to the Artist's Co-op. Alison was the first on her list of potential clients.

He didn't need to know that their agreement to keep their relationship light had kept her up for hours after he'd dropped her off at Flo's. Trey would have no trouble keeping his end of the bargain, she knew. It was second nature to men like him. But she'd have to keep her guard up. Not entertain any silly, girlish thoughts about love, not even when he smiled his devilish smile or flashed his baby blues.

They walked from the restaurant to the bank of elevators, and he punched the penthouse button. The next thing she knew she was standing in a small, bare foyer with a long hallway stretching out front. "So here we are. The penthouse, in all its naked glory."

At the moment, the only good thing she noticed about the expanse was the soft southern light pouring in from the bank of windows that cradled the foyer. The corridor was a bare canvas, neutral in color, devoid of personality. Her hands ached to touch the rough texture of the plastered walls. It thrilled her to know that her job was to breathe life into this almost industrial space. Her breath quickened in her chest. "So my room is situated in this wing too?"

"Sure is. Right next to mine. I set myself up here when I first came to the Nirvana. It gives me a chance to escape from my work a bit. And in your case, make going to work extremely convenient."

"We're the only people on this entire floor?" she said, taking a small, involuntary step back.

He grinned. "Does that bother you?"

If you mean, does it make my body tingle and my armpits sweat, then yes. "Of course not," she said.

Chapter Seven

A month's stay didn't warrant a lot of baggage, so it took only minutes to settle in: jeans and tops placed on a shelf in an enormous antique armoire; three sundresses hung in a walk-in closet the size of Flo's spare room; a grouping of toiletries placed on one end of the gleaming marble vanity. She popped open her laptop and plugged it into a conveniently placed Internet connection.

She stood in the center of the room and drank in the stunning view. Loon Lake sparkled like a sapphire, tempered by the deep green of the giant spruce trees rimming the shore. From up here, the fishing boats that dotted the water looked like little kids' plastic water toys bobbing in a bathtub. Talk about inspiration. Her thoughts flew to her first assignment—a written proposal outlining her vision, Trey'd said. His guided tour through the penthouse's twelve empty suites had ended at her door and had only heightened her excitement. She drew a long breath, dropped into a sumptuously upholstered computer chair and fired up her laptop.

Ideas sparked and took form as her fingertips tapped away at the keyboard. First of all, there would be no theme, no predictable repeat of color or form from room to room. The hallway, of course, would have symmetry of design, a sensible leading of the eye to a logical end. But when a visitor opened their suite's door they might be awash in creamy pastels and flowing fabrics or soothed by the monochromatic tones of contemporary design. No two rooms the same.

Delaney's fingers flew over the keyboard. The body of work of at least a dozen artists needed to be reviewed, she decided. She already had a partial list of potentials in her head, but tomorrow she'd need to hit the road and begin networking. *Would Trey be able to come too*, she wondered?

A smile pulled the corners of her lips upward, and she bent her head to the task. The next few hours slipped away without notice. Pages of detailed notes piled up in the printer's out tray.

Finally, her pace slowed, and she leaned back in her chair and kicked into the deep pile with her bare foot. Her eyes stared unseeingly at the beige walls as the chair rotated a full circle. Something special to anchor the end of the long hallway was needed. A large sculpture possibly, would draw and hold the eye, yet blend with the ragged, stone-faced cliff visible through the floor-to-ceiling window. She closed her eyes and pressed her fingertips to her temples and massaged deeply, hoping to be inspired.

Instead, she discovered that she was starving. She glanced at her watch. Two o'clock. Way past lunch.

She stood and stretched the kinks out of her neck and shoulders. In the bathroom she splashed cold water on her face before glancing in the mirror. The slightly flushed face smiling back broke into a grin. *If just poking a toe into the world of art again feels so right, imagine what Paris will do for me!*

Making her way back to the king-size bed, she sunk into a sea of down-filled pillows and reached for the menu resting on the end table. She was confident she could finish the outline for Trey by the end of the day—that is, after she refueled. Trey had said to order from room service or eat in any one of three downstairs restaurants. Really, could life get any sweeter?

She scrutinized the menu with a discerning eye. Now, will it be a crispy endive salad with imported blue cheese dressing? Or maybe chilled chicken on stone-ground bread with a side of pasta salad?

A single press of a button put her through.

"Yes, ma'am. Of course. Your order will be delivered in a few minutes," a polite voice on the other end of the phone informed her. "Would you care for anything else?"

"No, thank you. That will be all." And to think just yesterday she was wedged between stacks of old magazines and cardboard boxes of winter clothes in Flo's spare room facing down a plate of wieners and beans. And now, here she was ordering a gourmet lunch like she was a movie star or something. And best of all, she fully expected a dinner invitation from Trey to complete this perfect day.

Delaney eased the receiver back into its cradle before allowing a burst of happiness to bubble from her lips.

Trey clicked the *x* on the computer file and watched the screen power down, remembering to check the time flashing in the bottom corner of the screen before all went black. Six o'clock.

He'd just finished scanning Delaney's initial proposal for the project and he was impressed. Not only had she produced a comprehensive outline in her first day on the job, but her artistic vision was inspired. There was no doubt he'd chosen the right woman for the job.

His day had roared past, as they all did. He'd shot off the budget reports, payroll and staff evaluations to Head Office via cyberspace. His stiff neck attested to the long hours at his desk. Tipping his head back to ease the strain, he figured even his boss, workaholic Ethan Weatherall, would call it a day. Well, the old, pre-Lily Ethan, anyway. Since Ethan's marriage to Lily Greensly, his friend had changed dramatically. The fact that he and his bride were on a month-long honeymoon touring Europe testified to that fact. No more twelve-hour days for Ethan. Even the e-mails Ethan tossed off regularly from Europe were more of the touristy nature than anything else, with hardly a question about the state of affairs at the Nirvana.

Love, Trey decided, does crazy things to a man. Ethan was not the first of Trey's friends to put his career on the back burner for the love of a woman. Not that Lily wasn't great, because she was. But as far as Ethan was concerned marriage and babies could wait until a career peaked. Maybe in ten, fifteen years or so. . . .

His thoughts flew to Delaney and last night's pact. All fun, no ties. Now there was a woman with priorities he could relate to. Plus, the woman was a knockout.

He slid his chair closer to the desk. What should the perfect non-couple do tonight? He eyed the mass of papers covering his desk and extracted a brochure from the stack on the corner. He flipped to the section on activities and ran a pencil down the list. There it was. Dinner for two on Loon Lake. Perfect. He scanned for details. A large glass-bottomed boat gently ferried you around the lake while you dined on local fare. A pre-recorded tape explained the history of the lake's landmarks as you cruised quietly along the shoreline. Delaney would be far more entertaining than the tape, no doubt, filling him in on the local lore. She was bound to be more interesting than the stuff they'd dug from the history books when fleshing out the brochure.

He could just see her, dressed in a pretty sundress, her hair lifting off her face in the breeze, her full lips all pink and soft. . . . The pencil between his fingers snapped and flew across Ethan's office to land in a potted palm.

He wiped his palms on his thighs, reached for the phone and punched in her suite number.

Chapter Eight

Delaney and Trey leaned against the pontoon boat's railing. The night was postcard perfect, the sky blue-black and diamond-full. Loon Lake no longer shimmered, but lay in an almost reverent stillness. An early moon cut a narrow strip of yellow light across Greensly Bay. The lake rested in total darkness, except for the few cottage lights twinkling like fireflies along the shoreline.

Delaney turned toward Trey and smiled. "I'm so glad you thought of this."

"Me too," Trey said with a smile. "I can't believe I waited this long to try it out."

The first time? So he'd not been with another woman on this boat, looked up into the stars, shoulders touching? Surprised, but pleased, she said, "Me too."

"I guess an interim manager really should've checked it out before now. But I've been too busy settling in to the job and catching up on the paperwork."

The clatter of cutlery drew Delaney's attention to the tiny stainless steel galley at the rear of the boat. She watched with fascination as a white-coated chef prepared their dinner. Two juicy steaks sizzled on a mini grill, filling her nostrils with the mouthwatering aroma of the sauce's tangy spices. The chef smiled politely at her interest before turning discreetly away.

For the second time today, Delaney felt like an indulged princess.

She cleared her throat. "Lily told me about this boat, of course. Apparently Lily's committee, the Friends of Loon Lake, totally endorsed the environmentally friendly motor. You know Lily, the lake always comes first."

"Right. And good thing someone's watching out. We want Nirvana's visitors to be able to come back fifty years from now and still be able to fish and swim."

"Trust me, Trey, the lake isn't the only thing that will stay the same around here. Buttermilk Falls doesn't exactly embrace change of any kind. The whole town was in an uproar last year when the Ministry of Transportation insisted on traffic lights at Main and Water Street—the Bluebird Café's corner."

Trey laughed. "You're kidding me. Someone should write these things down. It's a whole other world out here."

"I know." A friendly, homey, suffocating world.

The boat chugged silently ahead. Trey reached for her hands and gently tugged them from the railing and warmed them between his palms. "So why did you set up shop here after graduating with a Fine Arts degree? You could've gone anywhere."

Delaney shifted her weight from one foot to another, but left her hands in his. Lily must have filled him in on her background. It made sense, really, considering Lily had recommended her for this job.

"You know, I didn't really plan on staying. But my parents decided to move to Calgary to be closer to their grandkids—and my brother. They offered to sell the house to me for practically peanuts. And I really hated to see a stranger move into our family home.

"My painting career was stalled. Derailed actually. But I was determined to put my degree to use. So I—"

"Hey, back up a bit. What do you mean your career was derailed?"

She'd only shared this bit of her life with her parents and Lily before, but the gentle lapping of the wake against the pontoon and Trey's evident understanding of the artist's world gave her confidence to speak. "After graduation and at my very first showing, the paintings that I'd poured my heart and soul into were given a horrible review by a renowned Toronto art critic. A man whose words I'd trusted."

"You must have felt terrible, Delaney. But that was only one man's opinion."

"You don't understand." She turned away and stared blindly at the distant shore. The spiky tops of a spruce stand blurred against the moonlit horizon as she blinked rapidly to bank back tears. "Nobody does, really."

"Probably not," he said.

His matter-of-fact words satisfied her. In making no attempt to minimize her pain with a perfunctory platitude, he'd shown respect.

"So what happened then?" he asked.

"So I rented the old five and dime shop and opened up the Art Gallery."

"Kudos on your business acumen, Delaney. Exactly what this little tourist town needed."

"Right, except the only time it operated in the black was the summertime."

"So, that explains the hairstyling salon."

"Exactly. I took the hairdressing course in Kingston and set up shop. My plan worked. And as they say, the rest is history. And as of last week, really history."

Trey was looking at her with something like pride on his face. "Good for you."

His compliment emboldened her to go on. "Most people around here think I'm crazy to close shop and move to Paris. Why ruin a good thing for a shot in the dark," she said, rolling her eyes for effect. Even her parents had tried to talk her out of making such a risky decision.

"Hey, life is all about risks. The people who take

them live bigger, rise higher, faster. And judging from the paintings stashed in your back room, you're not risking all that much. You've got talent."

Her heart flip-flopped. "Like that little peek the day of the auction told you that? What are you, some kind of psychic?" The slightly sarcastic tone she effected contradicted the goose bumps rippling down her forearms in anticipation of his answer. It was crazy how much she needed him to defend his position.

He released her hands and moved his to rest on her shoulders. "It's a gut thing." His smile faded, but his tone became more animated. "They drew me in immediately. I wanted to see more."

She lifted her chin to order to see his eyes. The clear truth she witnessed there told her to trust this man.

"Oh," she said, exhaling slowly. "Thank you. Too bad you didn't write art reviews for the national papers." It still made her sick to think how, four years ago, she'd allowed a mean-spirited critic to redirect her life.

The boat rocked gently as it crossed the wake from a small fishing boat, and her balance shifted. Instantly, strong arms circled her body to hold her steady. Up close and personal, he smelled of a sweet, musky cologne. *Why do all the guys around here smell like Dad's Aqua Velva, when this stuff is bottled and sold too?*

She turned her head toward the lake and Lily's tiny, rock-strewn property, Osprey Island.

"Did you know that's where Ethan proposed to Lily?" They both blurted out. Pulling apart, their laughter spilled overboard and traveled across the lake to a couple sharing drinks on a dock. Everyone waved.

"Lily says it was the best day of her life."

"Ethan too."

Men friends talked about stuff like that too? Interesting. They both fell silent for a moment.

"I think our best days are still ahead of us," Delaney said. "Me, showing my work at a prestigious gallery in Paris. You, I'm guessing, heading up some new supersize hotel somewhere exotic. Maybe developing a chain, the way Ethan created the Nirvana chain."

A smile stretched across his face. "You're good. Yeah. I'd love to head up a Weatherall group of my own."

He paced the boards of the tiny deck. "I've worked every job, from the bottom up, from busboy to lead marketing executive. I know the hotel business inside out. I live and breathe this stuff."

Delaney didn't doubt his words for a minute. Trey worked as hard as he played, according to Lily.

"I've taken on every assignment thrown at me. No matter where or when. Roland Weatherall knows he can count on me for just about anything, anywhere. There are not many executives in our corporation with that kind of flexibility."

"Sounds like you'd be the obvious choice," she said, caught up in his mood.

He stopped directly in front of her and placed his hands on the sides of her face. Her cheeks flamed hot under his touch. "I can almost taste it, Delaney."

His face moved closer. It wasn't cologne, she decided, his irresistible musky smell was aftershave. His lips brushed hers, softly, tentatively. The space between them disappeared. And then they were kissing.

One of his hands cradled the back of her head as his mouth explored her lips. He no longer smelled even a little bit like Flo's twin boys, but exactly like an amazingly provocative grown-up man.

She melted into his chest. Her arms crept up and around his neck. The motor's buzz, the steak's sizzle, the cry of the circling seagulls faded to background filler as she lost herself to the kiss.

By the time his hand slipped to the nape of her neck, to the small of her back, her ears were pounding with the heavy beat of her pulse. *Can he feel my heart thudding,* she wondered, *the way I feel his?*

Never before had a kiss electrified her senses, sparked her adrenalin like this one.

They lingered in each other's arms. The boat dipped and swayed gently as it rounded the end of the lake. The sultry evening air wrapped around their bodies like a smooth satin sheet, shielding them from intrusion.

As her heartbeat slowed her head cleared, and she realized she didn't want to move from his arms—or couldn't. Her brain directed her to step away but her body was having none of it.

She closed her eyes for a second, willing herself to step back from his body, hoping to weaken his effect.

Nothing. A second shift backward. Still no change. *For heaven's sake, my knees are actually weak.*

"Dinner is prepared," their chef intoned softly. "If you will kindly take your seats, I'll serve the first course."

With his hand burning a hole in the small of her back, they moved toward the linen-covered table for two set against one side of the boat. Trey pulled back her chair, and she settled in to admire the table setting. No shortcuts here. Fresh flowers in a heavy pewter vase anchored the cloth, flanked by two cut-brass lanterns from which light danced and flickered across their plates.

Delaney reached for her napkin and spread it across her lap. Looking up into Trey's face and beyond to the lake, shimmering beneath the early moon, she knew she'd never forget this magical night.

She looked again to the lake, her gaze following the low waves undulating from the rear of their boat to the blackened shapes of rock cluttering the shoreline. *Would a new life in Paris dim this memory?* she considered. Would the touch of his lips fade to become just a kiss, the stars just a bunch of constellations in the sky again?

She watched Trey for a moment as he talked with the chef. His gaze caught hers and he smiled, his eyes crinkling at the corners.

Paris better be all it's cracked up to be, she thought, reaching for her fork.

Chapter Nine

A spray of cool water pulsated down on Trey's head as he worked shampoo into his hair for the second time in the same day. His fingers attacked his scalp, creating a cap of frothy shampoo bubbles. *Women. Used to be they wanted a guy to fall hard for them, commit.*

After sharing a second, long kiss with Delaney at her suite's door, he'd strode down the hall to his own suite and headed straight for the bathroom.

Man, this was going to be a lot harder that he'd bargained on, he thought, slamming his palm against the faucet to shut off the water.

"Keep it light. Just a bit of fun, a couple of laughs. We'd even shook hands on the stupid pact," he mumbled to the empty room. He grabbed a bath towel and wrapped it around his waist.

And to make the matter even worse, Delaney seemed to be having no problem with holding up her end of the deal. What's up with that? Used to be women chased commitment, men chased women. But all through dinner she'd talked nonstop about Paris. How she couldn't wait to visit all the famous art museums and brunch at little cafés with other artisans. What did she call it? Oh yeah, *steeping in the ambience of art*. "Humph."

He plunked down in an overstuffed armchair placed conveniently near the floor-to-ceiling window and stared unseeingly through the glass. Knowing she was just on the other side of his suite's wall was killing him. But he'd better stay clear, he knew.

He considered his options and decided that having Delaney around for the remainder of the month was better than sticking it out without her. But if she knew what a hard time he was having keeping up his side of the deal and that it was taking everything he had to keep from charging over there, scooping her off her feet and into his arms, she'd run back to Flo and the twins.

But he hadn't counted on the attraction turning into. . . . whatever it was he was feeling tonight. Not just desire. Something he couldn't put a name to.

He sat up straighter and gave his head a shake. He grabbed his laptop from the ottoman and fired it up. The little red flag indicated he had e-mail. From Ethan, he guessed. He clicked on the icon. Sure enough.

Hey, Buddy,

Hope the Nirvana is still in one piece. Lily and I are leaving for sunny Morocco tomorrow. Bunking in at the Weatherall hotel for a few days and planning to check out the expansion plans with the manager. It's likely my father will call on your expertise there soon. You lucky son of a gun. Keep you posted. Let me know how you and Delaney are making out.

Ethan

Trey stared at the e-mail's last line and felt the hot flush of blood rushing to his face. How the heck did Ethan know about the kissing tonight? Had Delaney already e-mailed Lily? What had she said? He was breathing hard. Stupid Internet.

He squinted into the screen and reread the message, slowing when he reached the last line. Relief relaxed his shoulders, and he settled into the chair's pillowed back. *Get your head in the game, you idiot.* Like Ethan would even ask *that* question.

His breathing settled. That's it. Tomorrow he and Delaney had planned to visit a local artists' guild together. He'd focus on work. Be all business. And when he got back, he'd dig out his background material on the Moroccan job, just in case Weatherall Sr. calls. Regain perspective.

He snapped the laptop shut and rose, determined that tomorrow he'd have his head in the game. Just like

Delaney—in control, eyes on the prize. He drew himself up and sauntered toward the bed. Two could play this game.

Leaving Trey's shiny black Porsche parked in the underground garage, they headed north in the hotel's all-wheel-drive SUV. The dusty road circled Loon Lake in a seemingly haphazard fashion, the rough terrain dictating its winding route.

For a city boy Trey handled the narrow, graveled road like a pro, keeping to the far right on the sharp turns.

They passed no permanent homes, just a roadside corn stand set up at an intersection and a listing sugar shack resting in the shade of a grove of maples.

"It's the next left. Turn at the big red apple." She pointed at an enormous apple-shaped sign where the names of the studio artists were painted in bright primary colors. The sign stood out in a sea of plain, weathered cedar boards whose owners had neatly stenciled the name of their cottage retreat.

The road narrowed even more before opening to a flat, grassy parking lot.

Trey threw the vehicle in Park and turned to Delaney. "Now this is exactly why I hired you. An outsider could travel these back roads for days and never end up here."

Delaney reached for the door handle and smiled, happy that he was satisfied with her performance so far. After all, she was accepting an enormous salary from this man and intended to earn every cent. "Just wait until you see what's inside."

They walked toward the building. His arms swung easily at his sides, and she couldn't help but wonder why he seemed to be avoiding physical contact with her. She expected to feel the warmth of his hand on the small of her back, or a pat on the arm maybe, but he'd been reserved since they'd met earlier in the lobby. His tone certainly had been friendly, but not crossing the line to intimate.

Centered in a ring of spruce trees, a large prefabricated-style A-frame rose grandly from the dirt. The back door stood open. A small fan hanging in the doorway pushed a whiff of paint toward the car.

"The guild is made up of eight artists that share this studio. They alternate days, with four coming in at a time," Delaney said.

"They make a living from their work, way out here?" Trey pointed vaguely toward the trees and rocks that surrounded them. "Where's the market?"

"Co-ops are common in rural areas. This group operates a storefront in Tay Falls, a town about twenty miles from here. They take turns manning the store. And I managed to sell a bit in my art gallery as well."

Trey nodded his head in approval. "Super way to operate. Low overhead. No paid employees."

"Delaney!" A petite, redheaded woman dressed in jeans and a plaid shirt and covered with a coating of fine white dust beckoned them in from the doorway. "I was so sorry when I heard about the fire at your house. And the timing!"

"Alison! Great to see you again," she said, hugging her friend. "Yes, the fire was an annoying setback, but the cleaning crew will handle it as soon as they finish up the hospital." The day after the hospital's minor fire, she'd volunteered her services, but the hospital staff had politely informed her that they were flooded with offers of help and had alternatively suggested she donate to the hospital fund.

"Well, you wouldn't be here at the Co-op today if it wasn't for the fire, so I guess there is a silver lining behind every cloud."

Alison's optimism shone through words—and her work, Delaney recalled.

"I've brought my camera," she said, patting the leather bag looped over her shoulder. "I'm taking you up on your suggestion to take photos of the pieces."

Delaney introduced Trey all around and they began the tour. The room was an onslaught of color, making it hard to know where to look first.

Large, nubby tapestries hung high from the rafters like laundry on a clothesline. Rows of stoneware vases and free-form sculpture climbed from the floor on sturdy plank-and-cement block shelves. Closer to the lake-view windows, several easels supported works in progress. One, an ethereal landscape, the other a bold abstract of the same view. Delaney retrieved the camera from the case and took a few shots. Perfect for rooms 325 and 327.

Fired up by the abundance of possible purchases, Delaney spun around to face Trey. The undisguised admiration on his face assured her he was impressed. "So, what do you think?"

"I think you were dead-on in your proposal. This room is loaded with talent." His eyes darted from one exquisite piece to another, resting for a moment here and there before returning to her face. "Why don't you continue photographing and recording the pieces you want to buy," he said, nodding toward her camera and notepad. "I'm going to circle the room and pick out a few pieces for myself."

Well, that's a sign he knows talent when he sees it, Delaney considered. She remembered last evening and his praise for her own work and her chin lifted. She smiled toward Alison, clicked the end of her pen, and got down to business.

An hour later they settled into the SUV's bucket seats and Delaney took one last look at the solid, wooden studio. The thick walls of the plain structure held its secret well.

Did Trey feel the pull of the place too? She sneaked a peak in his direction. He was staring with displeasure at his nonoperational cell phone. She sighed. Okay, it was just her. Her gaze returned to the building.

"Why don't you paint here?" Trey asked.

Her body stiffened in defense. She'd answered that question, in various forms, too many times. It was embarrassing to admit that she was afraid to work beside these incredible artists who'd conquered their vulnerabilities and bravely allowed their work to be scrutinized by strangers.

"Been too busy, I guess. You know, making a living in my shop. That's why I'm leaving for Paris, remember? I've finally decided to make space for myself in my life. And you might find it interesting to note that most of the Co-op members aren't locals. It's common for artists to want to explore another world, step outside their box and escape what they know, in order to grow creatively."

His look was at first skeptical before softening to something more like disappointment. "I guess that makes sense," he said, turning to look out his window.

Silence hung heavy between them.

"I'm starving," he announced, breaking the awkward pause. "How about lunch?"

Happy to change the subject, she nodded her acceptance. "Sounds good to me. I only had time for coffee in my room this morning." She'd overslept and her plan to order up the continental breakfast had been scuttled.

"Let's hit the Bluebird Café," Trey said. "Tuesday is fish and chips, right?"

"Y-yes. It is." He'd only been in town for a couple of weeks and his office was just steps from the Nirvana's sumptuous buffet, yet he'd obviously been to the Bluebird at least a couple of times. Strange beast, this Trey Sullivan.

He popped a CD into the player, and she sat silently enjoying the soft, jazzy tunes as he expertly maneuvered the turns on the return trip.

"Look at that, a spot right by the door. It must be our lucky day," he said as he slid the SUV into the empty parking spot right in front of the Bluebird Café.

"Apparently so," she murmured as she reached for her purse and sneaked a peek toward the restaurant's front window. Sure enough, Hilda, the leader of the Gadabout Girls, was holding court at the largest table. A ring of blue-gray heads swiveled to check out the new arrivals.

Trey sprinted around the vehicle and opened her door, apparently unaware of the free show they were providing the townsfolk. She quickly edged past him and grabbed for the perky wooden squirrel that passed for a handle and pulled the door open.

A blast of warm, grease-laden air washed over her, reminding her of what she wouldn't be missing while in Paris. "There's an empty spot, Trey," she said, pointing to a small table in the back, near the washrooms.

Trey touched her elbow and steered her to the cluttered chrome-edged bar and a pair of stools. "Let's sit up front," he cajoled, "where all the action takes place."

"Sure why not?" Delaney plunked onto a plastic-covered turquoise stool and swiveled until her face was inches from his. "As long as you realize that sharing a meal at the Bluebird—in the Gadabouts' world—means we're just mere steps from the altar." This was exactly why she needed to escape from this town.

Trey studied her face. She knew it was pink, she could feel the flush. "So. Who cares? They're just a bunch of sweet old ladies." He flashed his movie star smile in their direction. He was rewarded with a round of coos and titters.

"Easy for you to say. You don't live here. You're mother doesn't chat on the phone with the ladies once a week." She knew her voice was rising. "You're leaving in a couple of weeks and won't have to deal with the fallout."

"The fallout?" He laughed out loud. "Oh, come on."

"I'm serious. They will say I probably drove you off because I'm too picky or something."

"You're picky, are you? I like that in a woman."

She grabbed for a menu and snapped it open. "You're missing the point."

He placed a hand on the top of her menu and gently pushed it lower until she was looking directly into his eyes. "No, I think you are."

His face was mere millimeters from hers, and he was no longer smiling. "What?" she said, through clenched teeth.

"You're leaving too, remember?" he said, matter-of-factly. "You don't have to worry about this stuff anymore."

His casual words were a splash of cold water. She sank into the cushioned seat. He was right. She was just a few weeks and a plane ticket away from complete anonymity. This relationship they'd forged, only a blip, a lighthearted frolic until their proverbial ship had sailed.

It didn't matter what anyone here in Buttermilk Falls thought after all. She turned to face the table of older women, feeling oddly sad and a wee bit guilty. Hadn't they fed her cookies and bandaged her knees when she was little? Weren't they entitled to a *few* proprietary feelings toward her?

She willed her lips into a slim smile and waved before turning back to the menu. She drew in a breath. "Okay. Point taken. Now, can we eat? I'm starving."

After they'd munched through generous portions of fish and chips at the Bluebird, they'd chatted about the weather, the hotel business, and the cost of gas. But Trey made no mention of another date. Had her appeal waned already? She settled her fork to her plate, her usual desire for the Bluebird's apple pie, absent.

Minutes later, after cleaning his plate, Trey signaled for the check. "We've both got lots to do."

Following his lead, Delaney pushed her stool away from the counter. "Can't wait to get at it, actually." Images of her morning's purchases filled her head, and she was anxious to return to the Nirvana. Hopefully the work would push Trey's indifference from her mind.

The short trip back to the Nirvana took only minutes. Trey wheeled the SUV around the hotel's circular drive, rather that park it in the rear garage.

"Here you go, Delaney," he said, "I know you've got a lot to do, so I'll just leave you to it. I've got a dinner meeting this evening in Toronto, so I'm off to the airport."

Feeling a bit like a piece of unnecessary baggage, Delaney quickly hopped out of the truck. "Absolutely," she said, raising her arm and waving the clipboard full of notes. "I can't wait to get up to the suites and mentally place these beauties." Did her enthusiastic tone hide her disappointment? She hoped so.

"Talk to you tomorrow, then," he said through the open window as he accelerated the vehicle down the hotel's drive.

She stood motionless on the curb, the canopied entrance sheltering her from the early afternoon heat. An all-night dinner? Twenty-four hours or more until she'd see him again. She turned slowly from the bright sunlight into the cooler tunnel of shadows and pushed her sunglasses to the top of her head. In the space of a few minutes, the expectation of her day slipped from exciting to ordinary.

Lily's comments about Trey's Toronto social life rushed back to her. Was the slow pace of Loon Lake living wearing thin already, and was his dinner associate a woman?

Of course, lots of his meetings would be with women, she rationalized—*and who cares anyway*—as she marched toward the gleaming glass and stainless steel doors.

She focused tightly on the bank of elevator doors and

forged through the lobby. The doors whooshed closed behind her as she fought for composure. This was just silly, she scolded herself and realized that she was more annoyed with herself than with Trey. Rationally, she understood he wasn't doing anything wrong. Of course a dinner meeting in Toronto meant staying over. Their kiss last night didn't mean anything serious was going on between them. He didn't need her permission to take off on an overnight trip or anything.

It was the realization that it mattered to her at all that disturbed her so much. She'd never been the type to sit by a phone waiting for a man to call or waste a perfectly good day pining for his presence. And after all, hadn't she been the one who'd demanded that he not press for anything more then a lighthearted summer dalliance?

The doors slid open and she stepped out into the small enclave. She'd stuck her hand into the depths of her purse and had begun rummaging for her key card when one of her mother's favorite sayings popped, maddeningly apropos, into her head: *Be careful what you ask for, you might just get it.*

Chapter Ten

Back in her suite, Delaney kicked off her sandals and quickly changed into a pair of cotton shorts, T-shirt, and running shoes. She tossed the saucy little sundress she'd donned earlier to the bottom of the laundry hamper, peeved that Trey hadn't said a word about her outfit today.

Each time they'd been together he'd commented on her appearance, often complimenting her choice of color or design. That was the great thing about Trey. When you were with him you felt like you were the only one in the room. But today, although completely focused on the job at hand, when it came to her, he seemed a bit distant.

She flopped down on the bed, realizing now that his mind had probably been on his upcoming dinner meeting. She flipped onto her stomach and with a desultory twist, turned her head to face the window. A wide shaft of midafternoon sun spilled into the room. She reached out a lazy hand toward the light and idly played with the rays. The warmth of the sun soothed her ruffled feathers. Things really weren't that bad. Didn't she have a great job and a ticket to Paris in her purse?

Bolstered, she sat up. *I'm a strong, independent woman who doesn't need a guy like Trey Sullivan. In fact, he's the last thing I need in my life right now.*

She rose, kicked off her shoes, and walked into the block of light leading toward the double French doors.

Here she was living the high life in a ritzy hotel, and what was she doing? Wasting a perfectly great day thinking about a man who in a month she'd probably never see again. How crazy was that?

Making her way to the glass doors, she swung them wide. She stepped out onto the oversize balcony and let her gaze travel the length of the far shoreline, eagerly absorbing color and form. The steel-clad peak of the A-frame poked through its stand of spruce, pinpointing the location of the art co-op. She recalled the artists, behind their easels, absorbed in capturing the scene with their paints and brushes.

A lump filled her throat, and for the second time that day, tears threatened.

Even as a child growing up on Lilac Street—two streets back from the lake's meandering shoreline—her attention had often been pulled from the tedious pages of calculus to the palette of color the lake reflected back to her hungry eyes. Each evening from her upstairs bedroom window, if she'd watched long enough, she'd witness Loon Lake's craggy gray cliffs darken to an impenetrable black wall.

Delaney shook her head and stepped closer to the railing. Her eyes roved the opposite shore searching for familiar landmarks. The lake was only a few hundred feet across and in the clear light she easily made out significant detail.

An oversized chunk of bleached driftwood, ensnared in a mat of twisted weeds, was snagged at the base of the soaring rock face. A stark beauty, a sculpture. One to rival those housed in a gallery's glass box, at least as far as she was concerned. Would Trey agree?

Her gaze moved eastward to the browning branches of a wind-damaged tamarack tree. Roots weakened by the nutrient-poor gravelly soil, it hung over the lake's edge, its tip caught in the stronger branches of a stalwart pine. In her mind's eye the stark geometric lines leapt to a canvas, a startling statement of survival against staggering odds.

Delaney threw back her shoulders, empowered by the scene in front of her. She was so lucky to be there, experiencing all of this. In a roundabout way, the fire the twins had set to her house actually had changed her life for the better. She flung her arms wide and tipped her head back. Her feet turned slowly against the balcony's smooth tiles. Anger and disappointment dissipated like fog on a sunny morning. She smiled into the wild blue and sucked in a breath of air pungent with pine.

Whether he'd intended to or not, Trey's cooling off had brought her to this moment and she was grateful.

Tomorrow was soon enough to tour the empty suites with her notes. She'd already put in the best part of the day.

Right now, she had something better to do.

His dinner meeting dragged on endlessly. John Westlake and Ian Blackley, two of the Weatherall Hotels' top marketing executives, had brought a lot to the table. They'd discussed the impending buyout of a smaller chain of hotels and the latest talks with the union.

But Trey couldn't help but think the conversation could have taken place via a conference call and through a couple of e-mails.

He looked around at the trendy restaurant. It was the type of venue he'd frequented whenever he worked in Toronto with its cutting-edge décor and gourmet food. He glanced across the table to John and Ian and wondered if this meeting was more about being spotted at the new hot spot in town than bringing him up to speed on business.

"What's up, Trey?" John said when Trey turned down a second round of drinks. "Used to turnin' in at sundown out there at the Nirvana? All that fishin' and whittlin' got y'all tuckered out?"

Trey knew John was trying to be funny, but tonight

his bad country-folk imitation came off a bit more mean-spirited than humorous.

Ian turned to face Trey. "Tell us, old buddy, how much longer can you hold out? You really took one for the team when you agreed to run the Nirvana till Ethan chooses a permanent manager." He winked at his friend. "That's why we cooked up this 'business dinner.'"

Cooked up? Trey felt his jaw tighten. He flew all the way here for sushi and martinis?

Ian continued talking, but his words bounced across the table like a Ping-Pong ball, not sticking long enough in his brain to register. "I was worried R.W. was going to send me out there to the boonies. Darlene would have killed me. I promised her I'd be around for the kids' soccer games this summer."

Trey shot his fingers through his hair and signaled for the waiter. He'd been tricked. Albeit, they thought they were doing him a favor. And truthfully, a couple of weeks ago he probably would have appreciated the ruse.

"Hold on, guys. It's not that bad out there. There is life beyond the Nirvana's walls." The teeming artist community, headed up by Delaney's good friend Alison, jumped to mind.

"Oh, come on, Trey," Ian said. "Nobody actually lives like that, at least not permanently." John and Ian exchanged amused glances. "Nobody you'd want to know anyway." The pair burst into laughter at the lame joke and began to gather up their papers. "Okay, since you're obviously done in, we'll call it a night."

Trey pushed back his chair. "Fine. I'll hit the down-town Weatherall and grab some sleep before flying out tomorrow. My new artistic director, Delaney Forbes, has a full day lined up for me."

Ian clicked shut his briefcase and grinned. "Delaney? Now that sounds interesting."

Blood rushed to his face. He never should have even mentioned her name. "Yeah, I've hired an assistant to help finish up the penthouse."

"Well, that explains a lot, my friend," said John. "Now we understand. She's probably good-looking. Leave it to you to find the only beauty in town and then have the good sense to hire her."

"Naw, guys," Trey said. "It's not like that." Well, it sort of was, but they didn't need to know the details.

John leaned in toward Trey. "So, anything you want to share with your buddies?" he said suggestively.

"Not that it's any of your business, but she is leaving for Paris in a couple of weeks, and I'll probably never see her again after that."

"So she's just another name in the infamous black book?"

Trey recalled the pact he and Delaney had struck on the terrace. They'd agreed to keep it light. Respect each other's career path. They hadn't actually said nonexclusive, but it was implied.

"Yeah, I guess so." A few days ago the no-strings-attached deal had sounded perfect. Tonight he was having trouble drumming up the same enthusiasm.

"You're a lucky man, Sullivan," Ian said. He looked at his friend and laughed. "Just don't screw it up by falling for her."

"Are you kidding? When was the last time I let a woman lead me around by the ear. I'm not like you two schmucks," he said, faux punching John in the shoulder.

"Hey, you're not invincible. We're just waiting for the day when you'll meet a woman who will change your tune."

They'd reached the sidewalk in front of the restaurant. Trey opened the door of a waiting cab and turned to John and Ian. "Don't hold your breath, guys. R.W.'s got me lined up for the Moroccan job. White beaches, long cool drinks, beautiful women—here I come."

He watched the two men make their way toward the underground parking lot as his taxi pulled away from the curb. He conjured up an image of the Moroccan hotel. A massive, gleaming white stucco castle, marble-tiled floors, rich tapestries, mouthwatering cuisine, easily the most luxurious hotel in the Weatherall chain.

And he was the lucky son of a gun who got to work there for a couple of months. He threw his head back against the backseat's headrest. Why did Delaney Forbes have to come along and change everything?

The hasty trip across town to her house had been too short for any second-guessing of the plan. She rummaged through her hallway closet, her hands landing instinctively on the stash of blank canvases she'd

Sue Gibson

placed there over four years before. She piled them beside her on the hall floor. Reaching deeper into the closet, she felt for the metal box that held her oils and brushes. The jumble of shoes and boots released their hold and the box fairly flew from the floor to her hands. She settled the container next to the canvases and headed toward the back door and the fresher air of the backyard. The faint acrid smell of smoke still lingered in the rooms, reminding her again how lucky she was to be installed at the Nirvana.

Quickly dialing the combination of the garden shed's lock, she swung open the squeaky door. A glance across the hedge confirmed that Flo wasn't at home. Delaney drew a sigh of relief and entered the shed. She was in a hurry and knew Flo's appearance on the scene would require an explanation. Why was she dragging out her old painting drop sheets? Was she going to paint something? Questions Delaney wasn't ready to answer just yet.

An hour later, an exhausted but excited Delaney stood on her suite's balcony, its terra-cotta-tiled floor draped with the drop sheet, clenching a number two paintbrush between her shaking fingers. Slowly, she drew a deep breath until her lungs could hold no more, before releasing an equally long exhale. She opened her eyes and turned to face down her past and a small, blank canvas.

She looked past the rail to the shore. The sun's light was paler now, the vivid colors from earlier were now subdued. She studied her loaded palette for a moment before dipping the bristles into a smear of color. Instinctively she knew exactly what she wanted to say with the paint. Her strokes were hurried but sure. Her heart pressed against her chest, filled to capacity with joy. Her hands flew. She was painting again and all fear of failure slipped away. This one was for her eyes only.

It was dusk when she finished. She stretched and twisted her aching arms until the stiffness eased. She was exhausted but happy. A rudimentary cleanup of the patio and stained hands, and then she hit the bed, fully clothed, and fell into a deep, dreamless sleep.

Chapter Eleven

Delaney woke at sunrise. At first, when the sun's weak rays began to seep into the darkness, lightening it to a hazy murkiness, she snuggled deeper into her comforter. The minutes ticked past and the sunlight strengthened, sharpening the images of her desk and chair against the backdrop of the room's beige walls.

Eventually she stretched her stiff limbs, reaching to corners of the huge bed. The morning air was still cool and she quickly cocooned back into the mattress, hugging her knees to her chest. The stubby cotton of yesterday's T-shirt felt rough and soiled against her skin, reminding her of why she'd dropped into bed fully dressed.

Her heartbeat quickened, and she jumped from the bed. She ran to the bathroom, pushed the door open, and flipped on the light switch. Would it be as she remembered it? Her eyes went directly to yesterday's work.

The small painting dominated the white tiled room, the colors singing Loon Lake's praises. Did she really create this? What she'd felt in her heart yesterday on the balcony was no longer abstract, but right in front of her on the canvas. She slumped against the doorjamb and let the painting's power wash over her. The painting was strong and sure. She smiled at the small canvas and pressed her hands to her chest as if to hold the joy of the scene in her heart. If only Lily were back to share in this moment.

Trey popped into her mind and her body immediately stiffened against the door frame. No, she decided almost immediately. Their previously clearly defined relationship was already muddied with unexpected emotions. She wasn't ready to share this most intimate and life-changing experience with Trey, a man whose opinion, she realized, mattered a great deal more to her than she was comfortable with.

An hour later, Delaney tossed a bunch of oversize pillows onto the floor of the unfurnished suite situated across the hall from her own. She plunked herself down and wriggled into the soft pile and reached for the Tim Hortons coffee cup she'd placed nearby. Room service had happily complied with her request, and delivered up her favorite coffee each morning. Jason, the young, eager busboy, had confided that many of the kitchen staff placed orders with him as well, when he did his assigned coffee run.

She took a sip. The smell of rich brew tingled in her nose and alerted her brain to the incoming stimulus. She sighed audibly. Perfect coffee. Perfect life. A perfect day to follow an almost perfect evening. The only thing that could have made last evening any better was if Trey had been moping about in the adjoining suite, wondering why she was unavailable.

She'd left the painting under the humming ceiling fan to continue drying when she'd crossed the hall to begin work, but it still called to her. She'd returned to the bathroom three more times and had stood transfixed each time by the landscape she'd painted so quickly.

Last evening she'd rolled up the drop cloth and stuffed it under the balcony's lounger. She'd turned on the fan, hoping to silently draw the oily smell of her work up and out of the room. No one need know anything about this, just yet.

Returning to face the job at hand, she knew she was smiling. She felt different. Better. Stronger.

The empty suite she'd chosen to start in was bright with sunshine. Too bright, she mused, shading her eyes with her hand as she faced the eastern window. She would need to look into finding blinds or drapes soon. Reaching for her clipboard she added the name of a seamstress who created one-of-a-kind window treatments. She'd give her a call later and set up an appointment.

She pressed the clipboard's clamp that held yesterday's

photos, and a cornucopia of color fluttered to the floor. Delaney sifted and selected snapshots of the artists' work, flipping each photo over to reveal the number she'd written on the back. Turning and twisting against the pillows, she held each picture up toward a bare wall. Tucking her chin to her chest, she scanned the list of available walls and surfaces and then carefully penciled in the number.

Methodically, she worked through the stack of photos, erasing numbers and reentering elsewhere. Like a puzzle, the pieces began to fit together to create harmony.

When satisfied with the room, she flopped against the pillows and settled the clipboard on her belly. Pleased with her work, she closed her eyes and tried to recall the layout of the suite across the hall. Was the closet placed on the north or south wall?

"Hey, you down there. Got room for a weary traveler looking for a soft place to rest his bones?" She knew instantly who'd entered the room. The sexy male voice sent a quiver through her body from head to toe. Trey was back.

Delaney twisted toward his voice and blinked into the streaming sun, her heart pounding. He was smiling broadly, and she was glad to see that the little dimple in his left cheek had returned along with his obvious good mood. Although, the lines etched on his face suggested he'd had a late night.

She jumped up, embarrassed to have been found resting on the floor. "Help yourself," she said, pointing to the jumble of pillows. "After all, you run the joint."

He waved away her suggestion. "Just kidding. I was just heading to my room when I noticed this door open." His gaze dropped to the photos. "Things working out the way you'd envisioned?"

"Even better, if that's possible." She wanted to tell him more. Like last night's inspiration for the sculpture pieces they needed. But he'd turned to the open doorway already.

"Must have been quite a dinner last night," she blurted out. "You look tired."

Trey hesitated for a moment as if considering his reply. *What was he pondering so carefully?* she wondered. It was a simple question.

"The dinner was relatively uneventful," he said eventually.

She shuffled the pack of photos she held in her hand. And that's man-speak for what? His dinner date didn't immediately yield to his charms? She waited for him to continue.

"I didn't sleep very well," he said, rubbing his temples.

She conjured up a look of sympathy. Personal feelings aside, he was still her boss.

"I'd forgotten how noisy the city is at night," he said, succumbing to a yawn.

"I know what you mean," she agreed, ridiculously relieved to hear the reason for his sleepless night. "I can't sleep through city sounds either. At least not until I've been there a couple of weeks, anyway."

"You know, the funny thing is, during my first week

here, I had my pillow over my head half the night. I even had to get up and close my window sometimes. Even up here," he said, waving his arms to indicate the penthouse level, "those croaking frogs that hang out in Greensly Bay drove me nuts. Not to mention that crazy bird that shows up at exactly eleven-oh-five every single night." Trey rolled his eyes for effect.

Delaney laughed. "The whip-poor-will. *I know*. You can set your clock by that bird. But, you won't be hearing it for much longer. They only sing like that during mating season."

Trey shook his head and grinned. "Oh, sure. Just when I've gotten used to it. I kinda like the darn bird now," he said, smiling sheepishly. "That song is a lullaby compared to the honking horns and sirens I put up with last night."

"Listening to the whip-poor-will while falling asleep is something I'll actually miss when I move to Paris," Delaney said, surprising even herself with the statement. Who knew? Buttermilk Falls had more good points than she realized.

"I'll miss a lot more than that when I leave," Trey said, catching up her hand.

Her fingers tingled at his touch. The old, flirty Trey is back, thought Delaney, feeling her smile widen. And now that she had her painting to keep her focused on Paris, she had nothing to worry about. She could safely enjoy their relationship again. She looked up at him from under her lashes. Would he kiss her again?

"So bring me up to speed," Trey said, apparently oblivious to her come-hither glance. "What's on our agenda today?"

Our agenda? So he was going to work with her again today? "You're free?"

"Absolutely. Looking forward to it. I promised Ethan this place would be ready in a month, and I always keep my word." His face looked as determined as his tone sounded.

"Well, I had an idea about a sculpture that I'd like to run by you. Had a bit of an inspiration last night, while out on my balcony." No need to mention her painting, just yet. "I noticed something that I think you might appreciate as well."

"Sounds intriguing. Lead the way to your balcony." He extended his arm toward the open door and the hallway.

Delaney hesitated. Would he catch a whiff of the paint? What if he wanted to use her bathroom? She wasn't ready for anyone to see her painting. Her heart pounded against her shirt as if she had just dashed up the stairs from the lobby.

He stood waiting as she chewed on her bottom lip. "Uh, you know, why don't we check it out from your balcony?"

He raised an eyebrow at her suggestion, a grin spreading across his face. "I thought you said—"

"I did but. . . . the view might be even better from your room. Yes. I bet it is." She ignored his quizzical look and hurried past him to the hallway. "Come on, let's get started. The day is half gone already."

"Whatever you say," he said, following her to his door. She stepped aside and waited while he swiped his card in the lock and pushed into the room.

They entered into a room almost identical to hers.

The now familiar smell of his aftershave drifted from his bathroom as they moved past the half-opened door. Shirts and pants lay strewn across the backs of chairs and hooked to door handles. Suddenly she felt embarrassed at forcing him to open up his personal space to her.

She glanced at him. He appeared relaxed and unaffected as he shoved aside a jumble of shoes that blocked their path to the French doors.

As they passed the small, round table tucked into the corner, she noticed the Monet reproduction Trey had purchased the day of her auction. He was right. The restful scene looked perfect in the breakfast nook.

"Sorry for the mess. I don't like the cleaning staff moving my stuff around. I actually have a system of sorts, believe it or not."

"Of course you do," Delaney said, shaking her head as she followed him across the room.

Stacks of papers and files littered every available surface, except for his perfectly made-up bed. I guess he lets the maid do that much, she decided. She pushed aside the unwelcome reminder that he'd spent a mysterious night in the city, not willing to let anything ruin her good mood. There would be time enough to stew about a man when she got to Paris. And by then hopefully Trey Sullivan would only be a fondly remembered flirtatious fling, already half-forgotten.

He pulled open the French doors and they stepped out into a perfect summer day. The air was balmy-soft against their bare arms, the type that made you want to stretch out in a lounge chair and let it warm you through to your bones.

"Now you're probably not going to believe this, Delaney," Trey said, smiling. "But this is the first time I've stepped foot on this side of these doors."

"You've got to be kidding!" She remembered him saying he'd never been on the dinner cruise either, until they'd gone together the other night. "What a colossal waste. People pay good money for a penthouse view." She spun around, her hands raised in mock disbelief. "And you," she pointed an accusing finger at him, "don't even bother looking out the window."

"It's complicated." He paused. "No wait. It's simple," he said, now looking directly into her eyes. "I stay at the best resorts in the world. This one included in that group, of course. But the thing is, after a while they all look pretty much the same." He cast a furtive glance over his shoulder before whispering. "Sometimes when I wake up in the morning, I forget which one I'm in."

His words made her feel sad. He was missing so much.

Then he smiled the killer smile again and said, "But that's why I hired you. To inject some personality into these suites. I want each room to be an experience, not just a place to lay your head."

His take on the seasoned traveler's point of view suddenly gave her job even more meaning. When she was finished with these suites they would exude personality.

"But as for the penthouse views and pleasure cruises around the lake and all the other features I help develop," he said, taking up her hand again, "they really only impact me when I experience it through someone else's eyes."

Her breath caught in her throat. His honesty robbed her of words. And the statement definitely tarnished the devil-may-care image he cultivated so adeptly. She studied his face. "So why do you stay in the business then?"

"Don't get me wrong. I love the hotel business. Buying up tired old hotels and upgrading them to Weatherall standards, or creating a new franchise like the Nirvana line, gets my juices pumping.

"I love working in the hotel industry, I'm just no good with downtime—being all touristy. I guess I have a short attention span or something."

She dropped her eyes from his. This wasn't news. He'd already told her, the day of her auction. At the time, his declaration had pleased her. He was a man who craved excitement and challenge. He liked a constant change of venue. It followed, she assumed, he preferred a constant change of women as well.

She steeled her spine. Well, she had other things to do with her life too. She dug deep to conjure up some of yesterday's joy. Her gaze flew to the opposite shore searching for a reminder.

Gone were yesterday's shadows and light. Missing were the delicate streaks of mauve and gray. She sought out the chunks of driftwood that had popped out against the rocky cliffs. She could barely locate them today with the clear, bright morning sun bouncing from the water. The lake rippled in a showy dance of color. Brilliantly white bubbles topped each ripple as the low waves traveled to shore. A couple of the Nirvana's small red and gray fishing boats were anchored off Osprey Island's shoal, undulating easily against their anchor lines. She drew in a deep breath. The view was breathtaking, in an entirely new way.

Did his work make him feel the same way? She glanced over at the man she was only just beginning to understand.

"Come with me and I'll tell you what I see, what it is about this view that inspired me last night."

They stepped closer to the outer edge and he settled his forearms on the wrought-iron railing. She stood next to him, her hands gripped together behind her back. Rocking from heel to toe, she studied the panorama spread before them once again.

Her fingers twitched involuntarily at her sides. Would she have time to paint again today? It wasn't likely. And she really did need to run the driftwood sculpture revelation by Trey before anything else.

She glanced toward him. His head turned slowly as his gaze followed the ragged cliffs directly across from their balcony then down to lake level and over to the bushy cattail stems proudly waving entrance to Greensly Bay at the far end of the lake.

"I see what you mean. It is amazing," he said. "Delaney, look!" he almost shouted. "There's a giant bird or something—standing right over there in the bay."

A gangly blue heron stood sentinel in the reeds. Delaney resisted teasing him on his city-boy reaction to one of eastern Ontario's most common birds. "That's Sam," she stated. "Lily and I named that old heron years ago. Dives for frogs every morning in that weedy spot."

"This," he said, raising his eyebrows in appreciation, "is spectacular." He shook his head. "I guess I never really looked at it before."

The breeze switched around, cooling the air. He moved behind her to buffer the wind, dropping his arms over her shoulders. The length of his body pressed against hers, his warmth seeping into her back. She melted into his heat, the quick beat of his heart pulsating against the nape of her neck. Simultaneously, they sighed.

"So what were you going to show me?" he said, his voice huskier than normal.

Show him? All she could think about was his body next to hers and how she longed to turn to look into his eyes.

She dragged her thoughts into line. Of course. The driftwood. With the sun's glare she could hardly make out the form of the driftwood against the rock base. Better to go directly to the source. She wanted her new find to make a good impression on the boss.

"Ah. I've changed my mind. Let's go out on the lake

for a closer look." Seeing the actual driftwood from a boat would be even better. A trip around the perimeter of the lake would be fun too.

"Anyway, I can see by your reaction, my take on the view is unnecessary," she said. "The view speaks for itself. And no one person could, or should, interpret for another."

"But isn't that what painters do? Interpret."

She felt herself stiffen in his arms. He couldn't possibly know she'd painted yesterday, could he?

"I guess so. But I can only paint my truth. Viewing a painting or any piece of art is a vicarious experience."

"Why don't you paint while you're here?" The question pierced the moment like a pin to a balloon.

She could feel his arm muscles tighten slightly, as if he anticipated she'd bolt at his question.

She wanted to tell him. Tell somebody. She'd even considering e-mailing Lily, just to release the experience from her brain. But she couldn't just yet. Trey, and Lily, would want to see her work.

"Hey, I'm here to buy other people's stuff, remember," she said, playfully elbowing him in the ribs. "I'll paint my heart out when I get to Paris."

He released her from his embrace and stepped back, "Oh, right. Paris. I'd forgotten."

So had she until the words had tumbled from her lips. The offshore breeze swirled across the tiles and around her ankles before rising to cool her calves, back, and neck—the very places Trey's body had warmed seconds before.

"But that's not for three weeks and we've got a lot to accomplish here first," she said brightly, banking back her gloomier thoughts. "How about you meet me at the dock in half an hour?"

He shot her a curious look. "The docks? I'm intrigued."

"Well, just keep an open mind, okay? Remember, we want the penthouse suites to be unique, surprising."

"Oh, now you've got me worried," he joked as they picked their way back through the clutter of his suite.

Delaney relaxed. This was better. In keeping with his lighter tone, she threw out a suggestion. "Since we're going to be out near Osprey Island, let's have a picnic lunch." It'd been years since she'd been on the tiny island, but every memory of the place was good. And for reasons she didn't care to dissect right now, she wanted to share the island with Trey.

"Sounds good to me," Trey said. "I'll call down to the kitchen and order a picnic basket. Meet you in thirty minutes."

As teenagers, she and Lily had spent countless lazy summer afternoons hanging out on the island, their lunches consisting mainly of peanut butter sandwiches and potato chips. No doubt, today's basket would be chock-full of gourmet goodies.

Delaney headed for the door and fought the urge to skip like a schoolgirl down the stretch of hallway between their suites. The old freewheeling Trey was back and she intended to enjoy every minute of him.

Chapter Twelve

It was almost noon when Trey descended the terrace's wide stone steps two at a time. With long, even strides he took on the graveled path that led him through a maze of well-tended flower beds until he emerged at the concrete pier. He pulled up short as the noonday sun bounced from the pier's impenetrable surface, stinging his unprotected eyes. Shifting the loaded picnic basket to his left hand, he reached to his back pocket and snapped a blue and white Blue Jay's cap onto his head and then paused to survey the postcard-perfect scene.

Tiny white gulls darted and dove above the fishing boats that dotted the bay, their calls piercing the Nirvana's midday calm. His eyes focused on a spiral of wood smoke rising and twisting above the fringe of spruce that lined the opposite shore. A burst of children's laughter from a distant cottage briefly returned his thoughts to his own childhood summers.

Trey stood a moment longer in the heat of the day, his eyes absorbing every detail: the sparkling water, the layered grey rock that rimmed the shore, the incredible breadth of forest surrounding the tiny lake. His feet rooted to the spot as the peace of the place enveloped him. Delaney grew up on the shores of this lake, yet she couldn't wait to get away, he considered. Was there someone, a man, waiting for her in Paris? Not according to the Bluebird Café set, but he supposed their sources could be misinformed.

He scanned the narrow dock. There she was, seated on a bench at the far end of the pier, sunning herself. He felt a smile pull at the corners of his mouth, and he let it happen. So what? He was happy to see her. There was nothing wrong with that.

Her long, tanned legs propped up on a bulky backpack, her head was tilted back, her eyes closed. A simple white T-shirt topped faded denim shorts, the shirt tied snuggly at belly-button level, the shorts, just short enough to make a grown man cry.

She must have heard his footsteps because she dropped her legs from their perch, slowly sat up, and with a fluid movement, slid the sunglasses from the top of her head to cover her eyes and peered in his direction. He swallowed hard. Man, this woman was pushing his resolve. Again.

The twenty yards of concrete between them stretched before him like a high school hallway lined with

cheerleaders. It had been years since he'd felt this nervous about approaching a woman. Sweat dampened the
back of his T-shirt as he soldiered on. He shifted the
square wicker basket to a more comfortable position
and raised his right hand in a wave.

She waved back. "Trey," she called out. "The lake's
like glass. No breeze whatsoever. How about we grab a
canoe instead of a motorboat?"

She was right. The morning wind had died down as
the temperature had climbed into the high eighties. If
he wasn't near the lake, the humidity alone would have
kept him indoors in air-conditioned comfort.

He glanced to the row of cedar-strip canoes tied
flotilla-like to a floating buoy line, each polished craft
protected from its neighbor by several bulky bumper
pads. "Sure," he agreed. "It's quiet out here today. It's a
shame to start up a motor if we don't need one."

Squatting, he reached out and snagged the lead rope
of the closest canoe and pulled it to the side of the dock.
Quickly untying the line he drew it closer to the dock
and settled the picnic basket in the narrow bow.

"There," he said, turning to direct Delaney to the
front bench seat. "I'll take the back. . . ."

He hadn't heard her approaching. But now the sweet
smell of coconut and a pair of long golden legs were
just inches from his face. Before he could drag his gaze
upward, she dropped to his level. A sheet of shiny black
hair swung across her face and he instinctively reached
over to tuck it behind her ear.

His insides tightened when she smiled prettily in thanks. "Need a hand?"

"No thanks. I've got it." *Got it bad for you,* he grudgingly admitted to himself.

"Be careful getting in, Delaney," he said, a gruffness deepening his voice.

"Thanks, Trey," she said, her voice full of suppressed laughter. "If we both manage to get in this thing without tipping it, then we're home free." She grabbed his hand for support and eased onto the front seat.

Even with a drawer full of Boy Scout badges to his name, he knew how easily they might be dumped into the lake. He glanced to the sky for inspiration and carefully maneuvered from the dock to the rear seat.

Breathing in a lungful of pine-scented air, he thanked his lucky stars for allowing him his manly pride and sunk the oak paddle to its hilt in the smooth water.

"So, where to?" Trey asked as they slipped past the end of the pier and headed toward open water. All he knew was that she planned on sharing yesterday's artistic revelation with him. He trusted that the boat trip would be worth his while. Any time spent with Delaney was well spent, as far as he was concerned.

"I don't know about you, but I'm starved," Delaney tossed over her shoulder. "Let's land on Osprey Island and eat before we scout out the shoreline."

"Sounds good to me. I've no idea what's in this basket, but I bet it's good." His mouth watered in anticipation.

In his hurry to get back to the Nirvana from Toronto, he'd skipped breakfast.

He stroked from side to side in an easy rhythm, covering the few hundred yards that lay between the pier and lunch.

The tiny rock-faced island, once slated to become a helipad for the hotel, still belonged to Lily Greensly Weatherall. Ethan had scrapped the helipad plan after Lily had opened his eyes and mind to an alternative choice.

Ethan eased the canoe toward a natural landing spot, a place where the smooth hump of rock sloped gently to meet the water. As soon as the tip of the bow scraped the granite, he reached for the length of rope that dangled conveniently from an overhanging branch. "I take it this is a popular spot."

"Lily and I tied that rope there years ago," she said, eyeing the weather-worn rope dubiously, "or maybe this is a replacement. Lots of people picnic here."

"Doesn't Lily mind?" If this was a city property, the perimeter would have been lined with chain-link fencing and posted with NO TRESPASSING signs.

"As long as no one leaves garbage or damages the tree, she's happy to have them here. You know Lily, Trey. She wants people to connect with nature, value its worth."

He nodded in agreement. It was true. Lily Greensly Weatherall loved nothing better then bringing converts over to the green side—his friend Ethan, a perfect example.

He rose and carefully stepped from the canoe, then retrieved the basket from the bow. Delaney grabbed his hand and hopped from the canoe with her backpack in tow. As he pulled the canoe higher onto the rock landing, Delaney stood with her hands on her hips surveying her surroundings.

"I still can't believe your hotel is here. Just a year ago that area," she pointed toward the imposing white building, "was covered by a grove of poplar and runaway with sumac."

"I know. I came out to the site with Ethan when the environmental studies were being done. Got to admit, the man has vision. At the time, I wasn't completely sold on his concept. You know—vacation in the wilds."

"And now?" She smiled, obviously anticipating his answer.

"And now, I think the man is brilliant. The demographic is eating it up."

She tipped her head to the side and tapped a fingertip against her cheek. "Would you say that you are typical of the demographic?"

He considered the criteria: ambitious, affluent, adventurous. Or as the guys in marketing called them, the "Triple A" people. "Yep. I fit the target." But had he picked the right answer? He watched her face for a sign. Somehow the conversation felt like a test.

"I see." She pursed her pretty pink lips. "So you occasionally need a break from your busy yet fulfilling life, and prefer something out of your comfort zone, unique."

"Y-yes." Why did he feel like she was talking about something other than a hotel destination?

She smiled brightly. "Just checking."

Trey deposited the picnic basket at her feet. "How about we eat now?" Women. Especially this one. He had no idea what she was talking about, but thought it best to distract her from this unfathomable discussion.

"Let's eat up there," Delaney said, pointing to a plateau in the smooth rock and a lone, towering spruce tree. "More likely to catch what little breeze there is up there."

She led the way, brushing aside the spindly juniper branches that intruded into their path. He followed, admiring her stamina as she plodded steadily upward. Those legs weren't just gorgeous, they were strong too.

He'd abandoned the hotel's treadmill after discovering—right out the Nirvana's back door—the dismantled railway line that loosely followed the curves of the lake. Apparently a local snowmobile club had taken over grooming the now defunct line and encouraged the locals to hike and jog on it in the summer months. A deer had surprised him one day. It'd sprung from the thick brush, its front legs tucked to its chest, clearing the path in a single, magnificent bound.

"Now that was worth it, don't you agree?" Delaney called out, lifting her arms to the cloudless sky. Like the tiny ballerina attached to the lid of his niece's jewelry box, her slender body pirouetted atop the granite. Unable to look away, he watched her sink gracefully to her knees and slip the pack from her shoulders.

"Wow." He executed a slower three-sixty, taking in the view. "You know, this little island looks so boring and lifeless from the shore, but once you get up here, it's incredible."

"I've been here a million times, and it never fails to impress me." Delaney pulled out a small fleece throw from her pack and spread it over the rock. "Have a seat," she said, patting the spot right next to her. "I can't wait to see what's in that basket."

He dropped beside her, noticing her fragrance, kind of vanilla-like. Too briefly, it tantalized his senses before dissipating. He leaned in slightly, hoping for more of the seductive scent. Delaney shot him a sideways glance and raised an inquisitive eyebrow.

Quickly turning toward the basket, he flipped open the hinged lid to reveal potato salad, seasoned cold chicken, bagels topped with strawberry cream cheese, and a selection of chilled juices. "Our chef never disappoints," he said, extracting two china plates and cutlery wrapped in white linen napkins.

In silence, they scooped from the plastic containers until their plates were loaded. Munching through the meal, they idly watched the buzz of activity across the lake at the Nirvana.

Tiny figures strolled about the gardens, pausing here and there to admire the pockets of multicolored flowers. The sun glinted off the Trillium Terrace's enormous stainless steel barbecue, the mouthwatering aroma rolling from the cooktop enticing the lunch crowd out of the pool. A young couple sporting matching life jackets released a second canoe, and amid loud bursts of laughter, clumsily paddled toward the mouth of Greensly Bay.

Delaney sighed. The hotel was a haven, a little piece of perfection in a busy world. No wonder they called it the Nirvana.

"You still think Paris has anything on this place?"

Trey's deep voice pulled her back to the island. Thrown by his loaded question—and he didn't even know about yesterday's painting yet—she took time to formulate her reply. Returning her plate to the empty basket, she leaned back slightly and placed her palms flat on the warm rock behind her. Yes, life was good here, but it wasn't a real life. Her amazing job, her huge salary, room service, moonlit cruises, all not real. None of them lasting more than a few weeks.

Was Paris better than this? "No, of course not. The Nirvana is a fabulous spot to holiday," she said, "as Paris will be, for a year. But remember, in my real life, I cut and permed hair all day and went home to mow the lawn and eat leftovers. This," she said, waving to the idyllic scene in front of them, "was not my reality."

"Point taken," he said. "I'm curious, what will you do when you return?"

She sat up straight again. Ah, that was the million-dollar question. A chill chased up her spine. "So much depends on Paris. If my work garners decent reviews in Paris, I'll probably get some notice from the big Canadian galleries. If that happens, I'll make Buttermilk

Falls my home base, and hopefully travel often." She laughed, but even to her own ears, it sounded half-hearted. "But, if I'm a flop in Paris, then I guess I'm looking for a new career. Again."

"I know you're not asking for my opinion, but the glimpse I had of your paintings the day of the auction made me want to see more." He spoke softly, his expression open and earnest.

Her heart fluttered in her chest. Should she show him yesterday's painting? She wanted to, but was still wary.

"I painted those years ago. I was still in university," she said, hoping he would just leave it at that. She sneaked a peak in his direction. He looked disappointed with her answer.

He inched closer and circled her shoulder with his arm. She snuggled into the warm weight of his body.

"You don't need to be afraid of me," he said. "I won't hurt you. And if you're worried that I won't be objective, you're wrong. I'm capable of separating my personal feelings from my professional ones."

She dropped her head to his shoulder and considered his words. Men must be made of different stuff, she decided. Or maybe, it was that artists were made of different stuff.

He couldn't know that she painted not only with a brush, but her heart and soul too. He didn't understand that any rejection of her work, couldn't help but spill over to her personally.

"Of course," she fibbed. "But just the same, let's not

confuse things. After I've worked in Paris for a while, I'll seek out a professional opinion."

"A professional! I'm crushed," he joked.

"Oh, stop. You know your stuff, that's clear. And I respect your opinion—you obviously have an art appreciation far beyond the average." She softened her tone. "I like hanging out with you. Let's not mess with a good thing."

"Okay," he said, his breath tickling her ear. "But just for the record, I'd say your talent is bankable, your commodity saleable. And remember, I was a business major long before I developed an interest in art."

He followed this statement with a slightly lopsided smile that tugged at her heartstrings. He was so darned charming. It was a shame not to enjoy this time together. She raised her face toward the sun's warm rays, inviting him to take the next step.

His lips settled to hers like they belonged there. Slowly the pressure increased, and she responded instinctively, her arms creeping up to circle his neck. The children's laughter, the cry of the gulls faded. There was only his kiss, deepening, demanding. Something inside her told her that it was safe to go on, and she gave over to the kiss. He explored her mouth with a hunger she eagerly reciprocated.

Through the thin cotton of his T-shirt, his heart thudded against her own. This kind of desire was new to her. Never before had a man's kisses made her want to melt into his chest, to stay safe in his arms forever.

A caution light flickered somewhere in her brain, reminding her of their pact to go their separate ways in a few short weeks.

She eased back, separating her burning lips from his. Tracing a finger down his jawline, she waited for her pulse to slow before speaking. He was quiet too, just holding her, no more. Once again the songbirds sang overhead as they flitted from branch to branch. A slight breeze swayed the tall spruce, cooling her bare skin. A spray of soft, little brown cones rained down, bouncing and scattering against the rock floor.

Trey's arm slid slowly from her shoulder and he rested his palms behind him on the rock. He looked relaxed, happy. *What was he thinking about?* she wondered.

A fishing boat buzzed by the island, its occupants waving a friendly greeting.

"The Hideaway," he read from the side of the small boat, "that's the old log lodge at the end of the bay, right? With the row of cabins along the shore?"

Apparently he was also electing to ignore the implication of the kiss. "Yes," she said, in a voice that sounded close to normal to her own ears. "Jared and Marion Greensly, Lily's parents, are the third generation of Greenslys to occupy the original log home." Glad to have something to take her mind of the kiss, to pull her back to reality, she continued, "The Hideaway is rustic, old-fashioned—you know, checkered curtains on the windows and a hand pump in the yard."

"That's where Emma, Ethan's sister, is staying until they get back from their honeymoon, isn't it?"

She nodded her reply. Kindhearted and generous, Jared and Marion were more than happy to look after their daughter's new sister-in-law, and able to care for her Down's syndrome and daily needs.

"I'd love to see the lodge sometime."

"It gets pretty hot, even out on the lake, in the afternoon; otherwise I'd say let's do it today. How about some evening, right after dinner? The lake will be calm. Makes canoeing easier," she said as she began to pack up the remains of their lunch. "I'm getting anxious to show you my idea. Still interested?"

She was starting to doubt herself. Would he think she was crazy to want to drag a dirty piece of driftwood through the gleaming corridors of the Nirvana and have it take center stage in the penthouse?

"I'm definitely interested," he said, catching her hands and pulling her up to a standing position. "Are you kidding?"

Into the wind, he flapped their picnic blanket clean, rolled it tightly, and stuffed it back into her pack. She liked the way he helped out, not leaving cleanup to her because she was the woman. A last glance around assured them they'd left Lily's island exactly as they'd found it.

He nodded in the direction of the canoe and grabbed her free hand, tugging her to him, then dropped a kiss on the tip of her nose. "Now take me to your muse."

Chapter Thirteen

Minutes later, their canoe rocked gently at the foot of the big rock face.

Yesterday, she'd painted its likeness on canvas with bold brush strokes of granite gray, striving to reproduce strength and permanence, but up close its features were less intimidating. A fuzzy coating of lichen, indiscernible at a distance, softened the jagged edges.

Undulating against the base, a tangled mat of seaweed and waterlogged branches served to root the soaring cliff into the depths of the lake.

"Right there!" Delaney said, pointing toward the large hunk of bleached root snagged by a broken cedar branch that hung over the lake. "That's it! The penthouse's feature piece."

She twisted her head around to judge Trey's reaction. Would he see it as art too?

Trey rested the paddle on his knee and looked toward the spot she indicated.

Nothing. He said absolutely nothing for what felt like an eternity. *Oh, no.* Her thoughts ramped his silence into criticism. *He thinks I've lost it. I've opened my artistic envelope too wide, and he is regretting ever hiring me.*

Her hands tightened their hold on the edge of her seat. Would he prefer a loon sculpture, commissioned from a big name artist? After all, images of the beautiful but utterly overexposed loon graced the walls and tabletops of hundreds of hotels and restaurants in rural Ontario. The loon had become an unofficial mascot. Not to mention, this lake was even called Loon Lake.

She stared at the rock wall, barely breathing.

"Are there more of these around the lake?" His tone sounded urgent, excited.

She raised her feet and clutched her shins tightly to her body and spun in her seat to face him. The slim craft rocked dangerously, dipping almost to the level of the water. Simultaneously, they grabbed for the cedar sides to regain equilibrium.

"Sorry," she giggled, after the canoe settled. "I know better than that, but I just had to see your expression."

His eyes sparkled like the lake that spread all around them. A smile broke across his face, as his head nodded an enthusiastic affirmation.

"I definitely see why you wanted me to come," he said. "The driftwood says it all. A perfect metaphor for the lake. Wildness, adventure, natural beauty."

"But will the Triple A demographic appreciate it too?" She knew the Triple As were a savvy, art-educated bunch.

"Hey, don't forget. I'm a Triple A. And I foresee this driftwood causing a big buzz with the guests."

"Trey, I'm thrilled you agree. I just knew in my heart this would work," she said, writing off her previous doubts as temporary jitters brought on by the responsibility of the new job.

Trey lowered his paddle and drew the canoe forward. In a gesture that appeared almost reverent, he reached up and stroked the wood's smooth surface.

Delaney could hardly believe her idea had solidified into form so quickly. "So, now what?"

"So, the next step is to bring this bad boy over to the hotel and have a closer look. Check for mold and insects."

Delaney's glance over to the Nirvana was partially blocked by Osprey Island's lone spruce. It's oddly spaced branches jutted out from the twisted trunk with no discernible pattern, the tree itself a worthy sculpture. Lily loved that old tree. Named it even, she remembered. She glanced back to the driftwood. Lonesome Mary?

"Don't move it just yet, Trey," she cautioned. "Even though it's dead, I'd feel better checking with Lily first.

Better make sure its departure won't disturb the shore-line's habitat," she paused and grinned, "or Lily's environmental apple cart."

She kidded Lily all the time about her passion to protect the lake, but actually was really very proud of her friend's commitment to preservation.

He rolled his eyes in deference to Lily, but his smile was conspiratorial, revealing dimples to die for. "You're right. Let's run it by our resident expert, just to be sure."

As much as Delaney would hate to abandon this particular artistic vision for the Nirvana, she knew, when your eyes were open to it, inspiration was all around really.

"As soon as we get back to the hotel, I'll e-mail Lily," she said, hoping that the honeymooners were on a break from their mutual lovefest, at least long enough to check their e-mail.

"Sounds good. I've got to catch up on some paperwork anyway. Let me know when you hear back, and we'll figure out the best way to transport it."

Working in tandem, they brought the canoe around to face the hotel and paddled the distance to the dock in silence.

Back at the dock they tossed their gear to the cement top. Trey quickly looped the canoe's rope to a peg on the dock and clamored out. Delaney grabbed his extended hand and clamored out, noting the tan on his arms had darkened since the day he'd come into her gallery. And he hadn't had his hair cut either, the razor-cut George

Clooney was beginning to fray along the neckline and over the ears. She decided she liked it that way.

Haircutting had never been a calling for her, only a paycheck.

Slinging her pack easily over one shoulder, he reached for the basket with one hand and caught up her hand with his other. Fingers looped, they sauntered the path back to the hotel's glass and steel front entrance.

"Hey, Mr. Sullivan. Great day isn't it?" Jason said, his gaze dropping to their linked hands as he hurried past carrying a tray laden with drinks and sandwiches.

"Sure is, Jason," Trey replied smoothly to his young protégé. "They don't get any better than this."

His words and a slight tightening of Trey's fingers around hers sent a flush of warmth to Delaney's cheeks even as they moved into the air-conditioned lobby.

The teak-paneled door to the manager's office was just to the left of the lobby, the elevator dead-ahead. "Well, I guess I'll see you later," Delaney murmured, punching the penthouse button. Something akin to loneliness washed over her. She didn't want to leave him just yet.

The doors slid open and she stepped inside. *Don't be an idiot,* she scolded herself. *He lives in the room beside you. You'll probably stumble into him a dozen times again today.*

"Hey, how about dinner in my suite tonight, Delaney?"

Goose bumps shot up her arm. His room? "Ah, what?" Now, that sounded sophisticated.

Trey grinned devilishly. "No, it's not what you're thinking."

Her warm flush exploded into a full-body hot flash. "Quiet," she whispered, well aware the lobby was full of curious eyes. She leaned closer. "I wasn't thinking anything."

"I thought it would be enlightening to spend a little time in the suites. Like a regular Nirvana guest." He raised his eyebrow and grinned. "I bet you didn't know that one-quarter of our guests order room service for dinner." He stepped into the elevator, still holding the door open. "Let's be them. Eat, talk, watch TV. . . ."

She smiled at his beguiling face. And she had to admit the idea had some merit. Walking in a typical guest's shoes for a bit could be helpful in taking the next step in decorating.

"Say yes," he said. "Think of it as work."

When Trey was around her, her job was never *work*. It was fun, fulfilling, exciting. "Okay. Dinner it is. Call me with the details." She tugged free of his hand and pushed him gently backward. "You're holding up the elevator."

He turned to face a family of five, all grinning at the tall man's determination to win over the lady, and strode toward his office.

Back in her room, Delaney headed straight for her computer. If Lily gave her the go-ahead, then they'd extricate the driftwood from the cedars and bring it up to the penthouse. She smiled at the thought of the wild piece actually crossing the lake and zooming to the top floor of the Nirvana.

With flying fingers she tapped out her message to Lily. After signing off, she padded across the thick carpet toward the bathroom. Her breath quickened as she reached for the door handle and then the light switch. Even under the harsh vanity lights, the painting stood up. She moved to sit on the edge of the tub, cocked her head to the side, and studied her work.

The scale might be a tad off in the right quarter, she decided, but not so much to skew the painting. Maybe another layer of cobalt blue near the horizon, she considered. Anticipation tightened her chest and instinctively— if seven years of yoga makes for instinct—she drew in and released a long breath. Soon, she knew. She would be in Paris and could paint to her heart's content.

She stood and caught her reflection in the mirror. Her usually smooth black hair was windblown, the sun had highlighted her cheekbones with pink. Her T-shirt sported a smear of spruce gum along the hemline, and her shorts were wrinkled.

She stared with dismay at her appearance. Not exactly the cosmopolitan image a worldly man like Trey admired.

Glancing to her painting and then back again to her image in the mirror, she pushed her shoulders back. *Who cares? I don't want Trey to fall for me. I want to leave this place in a couple of weeks with no regrets. Just fun memories.*

She snapped off the overhead light. If she kept telling herself so, it might be so.

Determined to stay on track—art first, Trey second—she left the bathroom and settled at her desk. The notes she'd made earlier that morning jogged her memory, and she reached for the phone.

Dialing quickly, she connected almost immediately with Kimberly Sampson, the seamstress Lily had hired to design her wedding dress. Kimberly was a whiz at creating one-of-a-kind items, whether it be clothing, linens, or draperies.

After a quick explanation of the situation, Kimberly eagerly accepted Delaney's invitation to pop by in a few days and check out the suites.

Delaney returned the phone to its cradle with a growing feeling of accomplishment. Her ideas were taking form, bits and pieces were coming together to create the vision she'd outlined for Trey. For the first time in five years she felt like she was in the right place doing the right thing. And yet she was still in Buttermilk Falls.

She sank back into the butter-soft leather of her computer chair and spun slowly to face the French doors. She allowed her gaze to drift, finally settling on the cotton-ball clouds floating in the clear blue sky. She sighed softly.

No, the Nirvana wasn't Paris, but it sure had its perks.

Chapter Fourteen

Forty-five minutes later, fueled by a foam-topped latte—delivered by Jason—and the day's successes, Delaney hurried to her walk-in closet and exchanged her shorts and T-shirt for white linen trousers and a jersey knit black halter top.

Popping a pair of oversize sunglasses to the top of her head, she grabbed her purse and sauntered back to the hallway and the elevator. She stood in the strip of sunshine that poured through the floor-to-ceiling window tapping her foot and watching the progress of the elevator's blinking buttons. She needed to get out of the hotel and gain some perspective. Big-time.

The short drive north on County Road 12 only took thirty minutes, and she was walking through the Co-op's brightly painted door. The room was dimmer than the street, with small lamps directing spots of light where it was needed. In the air, she detected the faint aroma of jasmine and remembered that Alison's ex-husband used to work for Indigo Incense. He'd gifted his wife with a palette of her favorite incense, right before quitting his job and heading for Vancouver Island's interior. And she hadn't seen him since.

"Delaney!" Alison, dressed up today in dark blue jeans and a paint-free tie-dyed shirt, flew across the room. Her waist-length red hair streamed behind her, making her appear ten years younger than her thirty-two years.

She hugged her friend. "I'm so happy so see you. I never got a chance to properly thank you for the huge order. It's just what the Co-op needed, a big injection of cash."

"You're more than welcome," Delaney said. "I'm just happy I get a chance to showcase everyone's work at the Nirvana. You and your members have worked too long without the recognition you deserve. I couldn't be happier for you."

She meant that with all her heart. These people were brave souls, trading regular paychecks for creative license. Respect and envy for Co-op alumni crowded her heart.

She scanned the walls of the store, taking inventory of the colorful paintings still waiting for a home. *Will I ever be brave enough to set my paintings out for critical review?* She studied Alison's smiling face, wide blue eyes set against pale, freckled skin. She didn't look tough, hardened.

It had to be like bringing a new baby home from the hospital and thinking it is the prettiest thing in the world and having someone ask why its face is all scrunched up. A shiver chased down her spine.

"Delaney, are you all right?"

"Great. Super," Delaney answered. "Ah, I just popped in to order another set of stoneware coasters. I miscalculated the number I needed." A phone call would have sufficed, but she really needed a reason to escape the Nirvana, gain a little perspective.

Alison smiled broadly. "For you, anything. I'm crazy busy, but I'll fit it in." Alison was one of the busiest artists in town, her pottery always in high demand. She'd been savvy enough to create an online store and now sold internationally. Many of the Co-op members were still struggling and looked to Alison for leadership.

Walking together around the store, they chatted about the escalating cost of art supplies and a new gallery opening in the city. Delaney often stopped to touch a soft, woven wool blanket or to stroke the smooth curves of a stone carving.

"So, what's the story with Trey?" Alison blurted out.

Delaney appreciated her friend's forthrightness. With Lily away, she needed a friend to talk to and had hoped she'd get a chance for some girl-talk today.

"Well, he's a really nice guy. Straightforward, honest. Makes-no-promises-he-can't-keep kinda guy."

"Oooh. Sounds like a keeper. Anything going on between you two?" Alison waved a finger back and forth in the air.

Heat crawled up Delaney's neck and spread across her cheeks. Her hand went to cover her suddenly tingling lips as she remembered their kiss under Osprey Island's big spruce. "Nothing serious. I guess you could say we're the proverbial ships passing in the night." Did she sound devil-may-care? She hoped so. "I'm off to Paris in a couple of weeks, and he's off to another Weatherall hotel. Maybe Morocco."

Alison stared at her, waiting. "So? All that written in stone or something?"

"No," she allowed. "But I've dreamt about this move to Paris for four long years, and I'm going. That's that," she said, brushing her hands together briskly.

Alison smiled and patted Delaney's shoulder. "All right. Just asking."

Alison's questions highlighted what Delaney already knew. A future with Trey sounded just about perfect. He really got her. And the attraction, well, enough said.

No, there wasn't any law keeping them from becoming a serious couple. Just a promise, and the fact that she didn't relish becoming someone's ball and chain. Trey had made it perfectly clear that he didn't want to be fenced in, as had she. Now was no time for her to go changing the rules.

The tiny brass bell hanging over the front door tinkled, heralding a customer's entrance. "I better get back," Delaney said. "Trey and I are pretending to be regular Nirvana customers tonight. Eating from room service, watching some TV. Trying on the suites for size and hoping to be inspired."

"To do what?"

Delaney blushed again at Alison's raised eyebrows and wicked smile. "Will you stop that? I mean *artistically* inspired. Sheesh."

Alison waved her off. "Call me soon. And thanks again."

The shop's door banged shut behind her and Delaney shoved her hand into her purse, rummaging for the keys to the small car she'd chosen earlier from the Nirvana's fleet. As her fingers closed around the cool metal of the keys, she wished she could pull out a big bag of resolve as well.

Like a movie trailer, a vision of the upcoming evening played in her mind. There she was nestled next to Trey on the sofa, the room lit only by the flickering television screen and the soft glow of lavender-scented candles. He'd pull her into his arms, scorch her soul with the ardor in his eyes, and beg her to stay with him forever.

The jangle of the shop's bell accompanied by the sweet rush of jasmine jolted her back to reality.

She slid the key into the lock and yanked the car door open. *I'm so in trouble!*

Chapter Fifteen

Trey stood in the middle of his suite and tried to see it through a woman's eye. Yeah, he was fairly sure it looked good. The maid had done a great job of cleaning up the place. His clothes were hung neatly in the closet, the bathroom smelled like pine trees and the desk was stripped of its stacks of paperwork.

To top it off, a platter of complimentary brownies sat cooling on the side table. The room no longer looked like a messy home away from home, but now resembled a typical suite.

Popping an entire brownie into his mouth, he flopped onto one corner of the small sofa and munched through it while staring into the television's black face. It occurred to him that he'd never once turned the thing on since moving in over two weeks ago. This acting like a regular tourist was going to be a bit of a stretch. Most evenings he was in his office catching up on paperwork and only used his room as a stopping off spot to change clothes or to catch up on his sleep.

He heard a soft rap on the door. He straightened his back and quickly shifted to the edge of the sofa cushion. She was here!

Four long strides brought him to the door. He paused at the mirror to check his teeth for smears of brownie. It was dumb how revved he was to be spending a quiet evening in with Delaney. Since when did a couple of hours of television beat out Toronto's night scene?

He reached for the door handle with ridiculous anticipation, knowing full well the answer stood on the other side of the door.

It wasn't a surprise that she looked great, but the crisp white pants and the black top made her look more sophisticated than usual. There was not a doubt in his mind that she would fit in perfectly with the fashionable Parisian women. "Come in," he said, stepping back to allow her to pass. "Hope you're up for this."

She shot him an apprehensive look, slid past him, and made her way down the short hall. "Up for what?"

Why did she always misinterpret his words? he wondered. But on second thought, he understood. Their attraction was almost palatable, coloring every conversation.

"Our experiment. You know. Brainstorming ideas of how to make these rooms special," he said.

"Of course. Sure. I knew that." Delaney walked to the French doors. "If I was just arriving, this is what I'd do first." She pushed open the doors. "First, I'd have a look at the lake, breathe in some fresh air."

She wasn't wasting any time getting down to work. "Good. I think you're right," he said, following her lead. "They've paid for one of the best rooms in the hotel, they'd want to check out the view." He crossed the room to join her and let his gaze rove over the thick fringe of evergreens circling the shimmering water.

Distracted by her perfume—tonight a sweet, flowery scent—he fought to stay in the moment.

When she spoke, it was softly. "Now, try to imagine that you've been planning this trip for a year. You've just come off a tough week at the office. You took a taxi, two planes, and the hotel shuttle to get here. Your feet are aching, you're pretty much exhausted."

He'd seen this tourist many times, so it was easy to imagine. Her whispered words seeped into his conscience. He could feel his shoulders droop and his fingers unfurl and he was pretty sure he sighed. *Man, this woman has amazing powers.*

She pressed a hand to his back and gently guided him to the balcony. Trusting her, he followed her lead.

"Now open your eyes, slowly."

The inky blue of the lake below drew his gaze down to its surface, eliminating any thoughts that remained of his day's work.

A pair of loons floated into view, their plaintive calls

reaching deep inside him to some primitive memory and sending a rash of goose bumps up his forearms. The air was still, thick with the scent of pine, and flowed like water across his bare face and arms. When he swallowed, the acrid pine scent slid down his throat, leaving a slightly bitter taste on his tongue. He rested his hands on the iron railing and drank in the scene like a thirsty man.

"Did you get what you paid for?" Delaney whispered.

Oh, she was good. Really good. "Oh, yeah. I'd book this room for next year's vacation right now."

"Good answer, Trey. Now we need to carry some of that beauty from out there to the actual suites."

"You mean more driftwood?"

She rolled her eyes and smiled at him. "No. Figuratively, not literally."

"Gotcha." Man, she was cute. "Now, let's go back in and get some of this down on paper."

Anxious to document their thoughts before anything brilliant was lost, he followed her inside. This was way better than he'd imagined. Some pretty amazing ideas could come out of this. And if not, settling on the sofa sounded equally as good.

She was already seated, her hair tucked prettily behind her ears. He grabbed a pad of yellow lined paper from his desk.

Close enough to smell her hair but not actually touch it, he poised his pen. How to put in words what he'd just experienced? He looked to his partner.

Her eyes shone and she bounced gently, like a kid, on the overstuffed sofa cushion. "Okay, take notes," she ordered with a smile. "How about every room has a painting of the view from their own balcony, whether it is the lake or the back view of the spruce ridge. Each one would be unique, yet a variation of a theme."

Caught up in her enthusiasm, he wrote rapidly until she paused for a breath. He dropped the pen and leaned into her and caught her flying hands. "We've already bought most of the artwork we need from the Co-op, but these paintings would be smaller, right? If we commissioned someone to paint them, I bet we'd have them finished in what, a couple of weeks?"

Delaney stilled in his grasp and he watched a range of emotions flit through her eyes. "That sounds about right, Trey." She untangled her impossibly long legs, rose, and crossed the room. With a flick of one long, elegant finger, she opened the tiny fridge and selected a soda.

He waited for her to return to him, to get swept up in her infectious enthusiasm again, but instead he felt shut off. *What had just happened here?*

"Want one?" She swiveled to look at him, holding up her frosty can.

"No thanks." She was watching him like a cat eyeing a mouse hole. She looked like she wanted to ask him something, but was holding back. The whole mood of the room shifted. He rose to join her, chucking the notepad onto the sofa.

He walked toward her until only inches separated

their faces. Backlit by the soft rays of moonlight, her face was in partial shadow, but he could see that her normally clear eyes fronted a storm within. Cautiously, he reached and tipped her face up to his. "Hey, what's up?"

Was that a flicker of fear in her eyes? He dropped his hand to his side and then looked away, confused. Was it him she feared?

She dropped her head. "I might know someone who could handle the job. That's all," she murmured, more to the room in general, than to him.

"What, one of your friends?" He spoke hesitantly, as if uncertain he should continue. "You've been bang-on so far. I completely trust your judgment."

She remained mute, twisting her hands together.

"Delaney," he repeated, "Who do you think we should hire?"

She felt ripped in half. If she took on the job and failed, then her dream of Paris would die right there in Buttermilk Falls. Why waste her time and hard-earned money on Paris if Trey, whose critical eye she'd come to trust, was unimpressed?

She glanced to the obviously confused man in front of her and wanted, so badly, to tell him about the painting stashed in her bathroom. Her knees felt like water as she battled with indecision. It was now or never. Trust this guy with her heart and soul, or give him the name of Josh Brennan, a prolific landscape artist who no doubt could do a perfectly adequate job.

She looked through the panes of the French doors. Each rectangular frame showcased a tiny panorama of the dramatic scene outside. Her eyes darted from frame to frame, fascinated with the individual story each portion told. She realized that not only could each room host a painting that replicated its particular view, but the tiny snippets would also make super post-cards to sell in the lobby. Just the kind of thing Trey would love to explore, she knew.

Clearing her throat, she moved to sit behind his desk and pulled the hotel's complimentary notepad front and center. If she was going to ask Trey for this incredible opportunity, she really should handle it in a businesslike manner. A profession proposal, free of personal preju-dice.

"Give me the job. Please, please," she pleaded. "It's perfect for me." She leaned across the desk, stretching her hands toward him. "I've lived and breathed this place for my whole life. You know I'll give it my all. I never hold back on anything I do."

The expression on his face morphed from shock to fascination before finally settling into a broad smile.

Emboldened, she charged ahead. *What the heck, I've burned all my bridges now anyway.* "I've already painted the view from my suite. It's stashed in my bath-room. Would you like to see it?"

Her words were out now, there was no going back. The numbers on the bedside's digital clock told her only minutes had passed since entering the room, yet everything had changed. Her personal relationship with Trey was now mixed in with a sticky business proposal. Exactly the kind of thing any skilled, successful businessman avoided whenever possible.

"Yes," he said.

With his words, a paralyzing rush of emotion swept over her. Relief, happiness, followed by a mouth-drying fear chased one another in dizzying progression. Her hand shook slightly as she returned the notepad to the corner of the desk. He'd said yes.

"The quick glimpse of your paintings I had on the day of your auction had me hooked. So," he continued, at a mind-boggling pace, "as much as I want to see your painting, it won't change a thing for me. Your passion, your vision, your picks so far have done nothing but convince me that I made the right decision in bringing you on board."

If only her heart would stop pounding in her ears so she could weigh and judge his words—to be sure.

"I would be honored to have your work hanging in the Nirvana—as would Ethan."

On shaking legs, she pushed the chair back and made her way around the desk. "Thank you, Trey. I won't let you down." Excitement pounded in her veins, making her restless. She could hardly wait for first light to break over the ridge. To paint dawn from one of the lakeside suites would be a perfect start to the project.

He held out his hand. "Now, take me to your painting," he said, reaching for her hand and leading the way toward the door.

Right now, she knew she'd happily follow him anywhere. And as for their stupid pact? As far as she was concerned everything had changed since that night on Trillium Terrace. For her, anyway.

There was no stopping the smile that broke over her face as she inventoried all that had happened in such a short time. She'd discovered she could paint again, right here in Buttermilk Falls. She'd discovered a man who made her laugh, who really got her, who shared her aversion to thinking inside the box.

She curled her fingers tightly around his as they approached her door. Lily and Ethan, the world's most unlikely, yet happiest couple, both took huge leaps of faith to be together, she reminded herself.

There was no denying it. She loved Trey Sullivan.

Chapter Sixteen

He slid Delaney's key card into the panel and pushed the door open. Stepped aside and placing a hand on the center of her back, he ushered her through the entryway. There was a lilt to her step, her shiny black hair swinging easily across the nape of her neck.

There was no denying it. He loved Delaney Forbes. It wasn't supposed to happen. He'd even suggested that dumb pact, swearing not to let it happen. But the fact of the matter was, he was crazy in love with Delaney. Just what he was going to do about it, he didn't have a clue.

"Have a seat," she said, indicating the sofa. "I'll get the painting."

She disappeared into the bathroom, clicking the door shut behind her. He heard a clatter of bottles and the sound of cupboard doors banging.

His gaze roamed around the room, settling for a moment each time it landed on a familiar Delaney-item. The scarf she'd tied around her ponytail when they'd canoed across the bay was looped on a chair's back, the flimsy gold-colored sandals she'd worn the night they'd danced in the Starlight Room peeped from under the edge of the bed. On the desk sat a small bottle of perfume, its tiny stopper lying beside it, as if she'd applied a drop or two as an afterthought as she was leaving to meet him.

Light from the bathroom suddenly flooded the hallway and she appeared. Her hands held something behind her back. She looked scared and he wanted to tell her she had nothing to fear. "Delaney, bring it over to the light," he urged, and reached to snap on the lamp.

Refusing to meet his gaze, she set the draped twelve-by-twelve square canvas on the end of the desk and against the wall. Immediately turning her back, she hurried through the open doors and out to the balcony.

Alone in the room, he was suddenly nervous. What if he didn't like it? He shook his head, refusing entry to the nasty thought.

Returning his attention to the painting, he whipped off the hand towel and stepped back to eyeball the piece.

Don't think of it as Delaney's work, he instructed himself. *Pretend you are in a studio. Opening night at a gallery in Toronto.* He closed his eyes and reopened them.

A small panoramic done mostly in blue and green

acrylics stood before him. At first glance the artist demonstrated well-executed perspective, skillful technique. He leaned in for a closer appraisal and the details of the work drew him in deeper. A scattered flock of tiny birds caught his attention. Flitting through a layer of thin cirrus clouds and just above the massive spruce trees, she'd sprinkled in a flock of small, brown sparrows, some diving into the spruce's outstretched arms, others darting in and soaring away in retreat in an apparent game of tag.

The trees stood in almost human stances. In particular, an old and gnarled spruce, its trunk seared by a lightning strike, stretched yards above the rest. Still strong, the tree appeared to be judging the junior ranks below it, sizing potential replacements as king of the forest.

Seconds ticked by. His eyes were seduced by an expanse of blue on the bottom third of the canvas. He knew the lake to be deep and she'd skillfully layered indigo, black, and a moody green to create the effect of an almost bottomless floor. Instinctively, he drew back a step and placed his hand on the chair back.

"Trey. You haven't said anything."

Delaney. She stood framed in the balcony's door. She was waiting, of course. Not completely ready to leave the story unfolding in front of him, it took concentrated effort to pull out of the picture and focus on her anxious face.

Her face looked pale. She was all vulnerability,

stripped of pretense. A new Delaney stood before him. An overwhelming urge to protect her rose in his chest. An artist took chances, laid everything on the line in a way he knew he'd never be asked to do in the corporate world.

She was the bravest person he'd ever met.

Grateful to have no awkward choice to make, no need to carefully select his words, he spoke. "Outstanding. Riveting. Full of passion."

Her eyes lit up, and she closed the space between them in an instant. "Thank you," she said in a husky voice, her hands grasping his forearms.

"I'm as close to speechless as you will ever see me. You've encapsulated the view beyond my expectations. The job is yours."

She squealed and catapulted into his arms. His arms circled her tightly and he swung her around, her hair a tumble of silk against his cheek.

Her delight at his words made him glad. Glad? That word wasn't big enough. His chest felt swelled, and he knew his smile would have to be sandblasted off his face. Man, if he could come up with something every day of the week to garner this reaction he'd do it, just to share her rush of happiness.

It'd been so easy too. He'd just told her the truth. He sobered slightly. If he'd experienced this reaction to her work, others would too. Big-time, actual art critics in Paris.

His gut tightened. If she went to Paris, he could lose

her. She'd get swept up in that world. No reason to remember him. After all, to Delaney, he was only a summer fling.

He looked at her face. She was still glowing from his reaction to her work and the job offer. Both propelling her closer to Paris, her dream.

He shifted to the edge of the sofa and scuffed a hand through his hair. He'd promised not to complicate all that with a declaration of love. He swore he wouldn't ever do anything to conflict her decision. Wasn't that why she'd made him promise to keep it light in the first place?

"Okay, then. That experiment definitely qualified as a huge success." He patted the seat cushion next to him and picked up the television remote. "Okay if we stay in your suite and watch some TV? Let's see what brilliant ideas we come up with over here."

She let his silly innuendo pass, too flabbergasted to respond. She wasn't ready to plop down in front the TV and order dinner from room service. Not yet anyway.

Showing him her painting was huge. Nobody had seen her work for years. She needed a moment to process all that had gone down.

She paced the small stretch of hallway while mentally checking off the events of the last few minutes. She'd fought her fear and had shown Trey her painting of the balcony's view. He'd loved it. She'd begged for the job of painting eleven more of them. He'd enthusiastically agreed.

These were big-time events. And now he wanted to watch television. Right now?

She eyed the back of his head as he flipped through the on-screen guide. A nice shaped head, normally full of intelligent thought, she decided, and topped with a crop of run-your-fingers-through-it, golden brown hair. On the nape of his neck, tiny hairs, bleached blond by the sun, traced downward and disappeared under his collar. His shoulders were broad, filling out his white polo T-shirt to perfection. She particularly enjoyed how the slight bulge of his biceps tightened the sleeve's narrow band as his arms lay stretched across the back of the sofa.

Well, maybe she could watch just a wee bit of television.

"What's your preference?" he called out, and nodded toward the selection of movie titles listed on the screen, "John Travolta or Brad Pitt?"

She nestled in under his outstretched arm. She preferred Trey Sullivan. His spontaneous, intelligent humor. His honesty. His kisses. His arm draped around her shoulders.

"Travolta, please. Remember, we watched a Brad Pitt movie on the plane this afternoon, dear," she said, following his playful lead. "I'm just glad to be at this beautiful resort. We so deserve this trip."

Tomorrow would be soon enough to deal with the semantics of her new job. Like how to fit in painting time and still take care of the rest of her duties.

But for tonight she was just going to enjoy Trey's company, order up some to-die-for room service meal, and thank her lucky stars for her good fortune.

It was all Lily's doing, really. Lily had sent Trey to her art auction in the first place. Delaney wondered if Lily had more in mind than an art sale for her best friend all along. Probably. After all, madly-in-love types were wont to fixing up their single friends and acquaintances.

Funny, a month ago, the very thought of Lily fixing her up with Ethan's right-hand man would have ticked her off. She snuggled in closer to his warmth, not the least bit annoyed with anybody. Funny how a thing called love changed a girl's viewpoint.

Chapter Seventeen

The next two weeks flew past in a happy blur. Rather than speculate on an uncertain future, if any at all, Delaney decided to just relax and enjoy every minute of her time with Trey.

Their workdays fell into an easy arrangement. Around eight each morning, Trey tapped on her door. She'd open it to a trolley laden with a yummy breakfast buffet. There were always two steaming mugs of Tim Hortons coffee and freshly squeezed juice, but after that, she never knew what they'd be feasting on: fluffy omelets, bagels from the Bluebird Café, crispy bacon and maple sausages or a homemade, fruity yogurt.

They'd eat, seated comfortably on the loveseat and discuss the progress and problems of the floor's transformation.

After breakfast and with Trey off to his main floor office, she'd work on the small landscapes.

The morning's easy rhythm left her feeling content, happy. They'd often lunch together too. Most days they would choose a quiet corner on the outdoor terrace, where they could discreetly examine a pencil drawing or check the budget's spreadsheet. After all, what vacationer wanted to be reminded of work?

Sometimes, if rushed, they'd grab a sandwich from the kitchen and sit in the lilac-hedged courtyard reserved for staff members.

Even though today was Saturday, she'd remained in her suite all morning, finishing up some loose ends. This "business" side of her job was tedious, and she tended to leave it to the last available minute. Unlike Trey, who settled in at his desk right away every morning and saved the more creative stuff for after lunch.

After phoning Alison to confirm the arrival of the last couple of pieces of sandstone sculpture, Delaney had eyeballed the long list of e-mails and sorted them according to priority. She quickly deleted the junk and spam, answering the messages from suppliers, artists, and friends according to date.

Lily was online again asking how the driftwood piece looked inside the hotel. She'd given her thumbs-up to the project earlier and wondered if there was a photo.

A couple of clicks and drags later and Lily's photo was soaring through cyberspace along with a pithy little note, thanking her for her expert advice and unwavering friendship.

Delaney let her head drop back and stretched her arms high above her head. Slowly she turned in her swivel chair and let her gaze drop to floor level. Her newly-framed oil paintings leaned against the neutral wall like holiday postcards, each declaring their particular spot to be the most beautiful.

Delaney slid from her seat and sat cross-legged in front of her work. Like a judge at a county fair eyeing a display of freshly baked pies, her eyes darted from painting to painting. Who could choose! It was like asking a mother to pick the favorite among her children.

She focused on her latest painting with a critical eye.

This vignette, a towering wall of limestone rising thirty-some feet from the hiking trail that lay just behind the hotel grounds, spoke of the rugged terrain's imposing beauty. She tipped her head sideways. Did her layers of gray and black paint create an imposing façade, like a fortress guarding the lake?

From the inhospitable rock wall sprouted bunches of twisted shrubbery, each branch loaded down with shiny red berries. Would anyone know they were smooth, not at all like a raspberry?

A fat crow, its claws clamped to a swaying stalk, greedily fed from the bounty. Would someone pick out the glint of aggression in its tiny eye?

Delaney inched across the carpet giving each piece its due. This wasn't work, she marveled once again, after reaching the last painting. This was a job made in heaven. To be paid to do what just came naturally was amazing.

Each day she'd approached her easel with anticipation, and the tiny landscapes had practically poured from her fingertips to the canvas.

As she'd worked her way through the suites, setting up in a new room every second day, there were times when she was sorry there were only twelve rooms on the top floor.

Even now, as she stood to select a small brush to use for signing the paintings, she brushed away the tantalizing thought that kept popping into her head. She didn't have to stop painting the local countryside when the last commissioned painting was finished. It wasn't written in stone that she go to Paris.

She snatched up her palette and dipped her brush into the black paint. Kneeling again, she began adding her initials to the bottom right of each canvas.

Up until a few weeks ago, she needed to be in Paris, a distant, yet inspiring place to prove her artistic talent. But now that she'd faced down her demons and produced close to a dozen paintings, her reason for leaving Buttermilk Falls was fading fast. In fact, over the past two weeks, Alison had repeatedly urged her to join the Co-op.

Delaney's paintbrush stilled, and she stared unseeingly at the waiting canvas. Was a career in Paris, by necessity, a better career than one based on the shores of Loon Lake? Up until lately, she'd always thought so.

Then, of course, there was her irresistible boss. Tipping her head to the side, she pictured his smile and the way that it crinkled the corners of his eyes.

Jumping up, she returned to her desk and tossed the tiny brush into the cleaner. She reached for a pencil and began sketching the strong lines of Trey's face on to a blank piece of paper clipped to the top of her easel.

He smiled a lot, she thought, her pencil flying across the paper trying to capture the turn of his lips. And why not? The world lay at his feet. Travel, excitement.

Trey certainly acted like a man enjoying his time at Loon Lake. The latter thought brought a smile to her lips as she recalled last night's good-night kiss. It had been long and luscious, only ending when the bell of the elevator signaled the arrival of the cleaning staff.

She turned her wrist to check the time. Ten to twelve. Tossing the pencil aside, she dashed for the bathroom. Trey was always on time and several times already this week, he'd caught her paint-smeared and smelling of turpentine. Not that it seemed to matter to him. He'd pull her into his arms for a hug and kiss anyway.

She glanced in the mirror. Her shoulder-length hair was caught up in a slightly messy ponytail. One strap of her once-white overalls dangled down her front. The narrow, baby blue tube top she wore underneath sported a mix of pale yellow and red smears from yesterday's work.

Yanking the ponytail elastic from her hair, it tumbled free, and she realized that Trey wasn't the only one who could use a trim. No time for a makeup job, she settled for a smear of pink lip gloss over her lips.

Not enough time to change either, so lunch would have to be in the suite or out back in the kitchen garden again today.

Her heart sped up with his familiar knock and it was all she could do to keep from skipping like a schoolgirl on her way to answer the door.

"Hi there, beautiful," Trey said, smiling his crinkly smile. Before she knew it, she was being tugged into his arms. He dropped a friendly kiss on the tip on her nose. Tilting her head to return his greeting, her words stuck in her throat. Instead of a jovial twinkle, his eyes were dark, almost sorrowful.

Was he feeling the same bittersweet happiness as she was? It was unsettling to feel so happy yet sad at the same time. Things were good between them. Really good. She thought about him night and day. She thought about seeing him again the second he dropped her at the door.

But could she tell him? Would he tell her? They'd sworn they wouldn't go there.

And did she really want to go there? Once she laid her feelings bare, it would irrevocably change everything, for both of them.

Instead, she pressed her cheek into the lapel of his Armani suit. She didn't need the discreet monogram stitched to the pocket to know it was expensive, the smooth texture and fine stitching was enough. She also knew that the men who wore this uniform didn't languish for long on the shores of a backwater lake.

Briefly, she tightened her arms about his neck before dropping back to her heels.

"Hi yourself," she finally said, admiring his freshly-shaven face. "Don't you look all the big-time corporate tycoon today."

He shrugged off the compliment, a blush of color seeping above his shirt collar. "Met with my accounting team from the head office this morning. They just took the van back over to the airport. Not a moment too soon either," he said, folding her hand into his. "I was afraid they were going to run over into our lunchtime."

Our lunchtime. It was her turn to feel a flush of warmth at his proprietary words. Were these the words of a man sworn to avoid commitment? Hope flared in her heart. Could he be having second thoughts about the pact too?

"Like I'd eat lunch without you?" she joked, instead of acknowledging the elephant in the room. "You're the one with the free pass to the kitchen."

"That's true. But I wasn't worried about that. I figured out a long time ago that the way to your heart is through your stomach."

"Smart man." *My heart? I thought hearts were off the table? It's just an expression,* she reminded herself, but as if it had a mind of its own, her body swung to face him again.

"Delaney?" he said softly.

Her heart thudded in her chest. "What?"

"Do you remember the night we made our deal about keeping things . . . er . . . light?"

"Sure," she said as lightly as she could muster. She'd thought of practically nothing else except their impulsive pact for days. "Big relief when we discovered that we were on the same page, remember."

His expression was inscrutable.

"Back then," she threw the two words out like a politician's spin doctor releasing a trial balloon.

"Yeah. Sure was a relief. . . ." His words tapered off.

She stared at the carpet. The happy voices of children swimming in the outdoor pool drifted through the partially opened balcony door while she waited for more words.

She raised her head slowly. Maybe there wasn't any more?

Finally his deep voice broke the silence. "Back then."

Her limbs loosened, her breath released. She smiled. "Oh."

Okay, here was her big chance. Should she admit she wanted more than a summer fling? That she didn't even need Paris anymore. That because of his trust in her talent, her frightened muse had come out of hiding. She now knew that love didn't smother a muse, it fed its hunger.

The lump in her throat grew bigger, and her chest felt constricted. *A really bad time to have a heart attack,* she considered.

Suddenly, his chest vibrated under her cheek. She leapt back.

He shot her a look of confusion, as his hand disappeared into his breast pocket. Extracting a slim cell phone, he flipped it open. "Sullivan here."

"Mr. Weatherall!" He straightened his shoulders and turned his body slightly toward the door. His face grew animated as he listened to voice on the other end, obviously the senior Weatherall, majority owner of the international hotel chain.

"Yes, sir. I understand. I'll look forward to it. And thank you. You won't be disappointed." He snapped closed the phone, his movie star smile firmly back in place.

The mood broken, she acknowledged the interruption that had completely derailed their personal conversation. "What's up?" she asked brightly, rallying up a smile while bemoaning the invention of the cell phone.

"Good news. Roland Weatherall is coming here for the grand opening of the penthouse—Friday. With loads of press, too."

"Press?"

He paced the carpeted hallway. "Big opportunity for the hotel here," he said, his arms spread wide to back up his statement. Suddenly his eyes focused tightly on her face. "Can you have everything in place in six days?"

She clenched her hands behind her back and banked down her panic. Forcing herself to focus, she ran an inventory of to-do's through her mind. "I think so. I've only got two landscapes left to do. All of our orders from Alison and Kimberly are here. I just need to do some fine-tuning on arrangement—and your guys to place the furniture."

"Great." He pulled out his phone again. "Excuse me, Delaney. I need to get on this right now. Better skip lunch too. Dinner okay?"

"Sure." So much for handing over her heart and accepting his romantic declaration of love.

She turned and walked toward her easel. The rudimentary sketch of Trey's face clipped to the top waved in the lake breeze, a tiny banner declaring her hidden feelings. She snatched the paper and scrunched it into a ball.

Suddenly he was back, his big hands circling her waist. Picking her up off the floor he swung her easily around in a circle. "Do you realize what great news this is for both of us? My boss is about to realize that this Nirvana is the best of the chain and your landscapes are going to get national attention."

Good news? Then why did her knees feel like water?

Snooty, mean-spirited art critics schooled in the fine art of crushing dreams were about to swarm her tiny little paintings.

Anger flared from the spark of fear that lived in her gut. "Maybe I don't want that kind of attention. What do any of them know about this place? The reasons I paint are personal."

Trey's smile faded. "I thought you'd be pleased." A

look of confusion muddied the bright glow of his eyes. "These guys are read and respected by gallery owners and buyers everywhere. Their 'discoveries' often become overnight sensations."

"Or never work again."

Trey's hands dropped to his sides, his look of confusion slowly clearing. His hands reached out for her, but she dropped hers to her sides.

"Delaney. I'm sorry," he said, his tender voice bringing the pinprick of tears to her eyes. "I know this must bring up some awful memories."

Instantly she regretted lashing out at him. He'd meant well.

She conjured up a smile. He'd nothing to be sorry for, she knew. But she desperately needed time to think. More air in the room, even. "No, I apologize. I'm overreacting. You know me. I hear 'art critic' and I go all crazy."

He didn't budge, his sympathetic gaze trained on her face.

"Go ahead." She waved and nodded toward the door, focusing on a spot just below his chin. "We both have tons to do. I'll catch up with you at dinner, okay?"

"All right." He reached for the doorknob and backed out of the room. "But I don't want you worrying all day. Remember, I'm proud to have your work hanging on these walls. Trust me on this, will you?"

She nodded and pushed her smile wider. *Trust him?* No matter what he said, she wasn't convinced Trey could be entirely impartial anymore. She'd trusted her art professor when he'd encouraged her to show her work at a trendy gallery. After that devastating experience, she'd put down her paintbrushes for over five years.

Did she have reason to be scared? Darn right she did.

Chapter Eighteen

The penthouse floor was a flurry of activity for the rest of the week, with Roland Weatherall's visit exploding into a full-fledged gala.

Delaney and Trey had worked long into the evening for the past six days, making sure every detail was perfect. Up near dawn every day, they worked through lunch most days and generally ate dinner with their crew of helpers.

If Trey wanted to dissolve the pact, he'd have to wait until after the gala.

Delaney had no doubt the response to the penthouse would be positive. She and Trey had worked together like a well-oiled machine, determined to break new ground in the hotel interiors business.

But the response to her tiny oils in particular? A shiver slid up her backbone. Who knew?

Trey thought he did. The heavenly aroma filling her suite pulled her gaze to the roses delivered an hour before. Trey had written on the attached note: *Tonight the world will discover what only I have been privileged to see.*

She closed her suite's door behind her and gathered her ice-blue, billowing skirt into her gloved hands. Lifting it a few inches off the gleaming slate, she stood for a moment admiring the hallway. What a transformation from the echoing, beige passageway Trey had shown her a month ago.

The walls, now terra-cotta, created a warm, welcoming feel. Recessed lighting brightened the space without slowing the eye in its procession to the far end.

She paused and looked at the massive, polished driftwood sculpture perched on a wrought-iron pedestal placed in front of the expansive end window. She drew in a breath. Exactly as she'd intended, it set the tone for the entire wing: clean, natural, exciting, groundbreaking.

The ping of the rising elevator broke into her thoughts, and she hurried toward the tiny foyer, the soft swishing of her voluminous dress the only sound on the penthouse floor.

Her fingers tightened their hold on her tiny clutch purse, and her chest constricted. She glanced back at her locked door. She could always say she was sick.

She eyed the flashing light on top of the elevator door. Trey was in there, she knew.

No. She'd stick it out. He'd never forgive her for

bailing, especially since his boss, Mr. Weatherall Sr., was in attendance.

The doors slid apart. Trey, looking every bit the successful hotelier and obviously in his comfort zone, was dressed in a black tux. He stepped out, ahead of the crowd, and reached for her hand. Smiling a conspiratorial smile, he swung her to face the sea of suits and shimmering gowns.

Pasting a smile on her face, Delaney began to shake hands politely with the elite group of financiers and hotel magnates. Next, reporters and art critics from the national papers swarmed the passageway.

Her eyes anxiously scanned the name tags the press wore on their left shoulder. Was Noah Cravet here?

"Delaney Forbes!"

She turned to face Britney Carlisle, a style columnist based out of Montreal. "Britney. Great to see you." They'd attended university together and last Delaney had heard, Britney was making a name for herself in the booming industry of home décor.

"I wouldn't miss the opening of this wing for anything, girl," she said, lifting her glass of champagne in salute to her friend. "The buzz about your collaboration with Trey Sullivan is hot, hot, hot!"

Heat rushed to her cheeks and she stared at Britney's perfectly made up face. How could she possibly know about her and Trey? She could barely hear Britney's next words her heartbeat was thumping so loudly in her ears.

"It's all the talk. You know. How Trey orchestrated the initial design stages and how you took his vision and brought it to life."

Of course. Britney meant their teamwork. Her heart rate slowed to somewhere near normal. "Really?"

She wondered how word of their collaboration got out. Britney's effusive take may have been a bit over the top but for the most part, her information was bang-on. From the day Trey stepped into her art sale he'd known what he wanted, and it had been a joy to help him flesh it out and find the artwork.

"The design insiders are saying you two are ushering in a new age of hotel décor. Shaking up the industry."

"You're kidding?" Hotel décor was a specialized industry? It continually amazed her at how much she had to learn about the hotel biz.

"Well, I better get to work," Britney said, fishing a notebook and small digital camera from her designer purse. "Talk to you later."

Delaney leaned against the cool plastered wall for a moment, catching her breath. The milling group had thinned as the attendees disappeared into the suites, only to reappear minutes later and enter another. A steady hum of conversation filled the air, punctuated with higher-pitched oohs and ahhs.

"So what do you think?" It was Trey, back at her side. Excitement filled his words. It was no wonder he loved his work so much. Tonight was huge payback for his long hours and dedication.

"I'm thrilled. Blown away." She leaned into his arm. "Scared."

"I know. But if it helps, I overheard an art reporter talking about your paintings. He said your paintings were miniature masterpieces and that you brought a little piece of the outdoors inside to each suite."

Her knees began to shake. "Who? Who said that?" She scanned the hallway needing to put a face to the quote.

Trey nodded to a portly man scribbling notes on a yellow pad. "Richard Brown from *The Chronicle*."

Delaney knew his column. He was the real deal. Tears of happiness threatened her composure further. "Trey, I can't believe it! You have no idea what this means to me."

"I think I do," he whispered into her hair. "This summer I discovered that you paint from your heart. It's more than what you do, it's who you are."

She blinked back tears for a second time, hoping her mascara was still in place. He really did get her.

"And how about you? Has Mr. Weatherall said anything to you about your next project?" she asked in a bright tone, belying her true feeling about Trey's impending departure from Buttermilk Falls.

"Not yet. He'll probably give me my assignment tomorrow after all the hoopla dies down." He threw his arm around her shoulders and pressed her body next to his side before going on. "Right now I'm just happy to be by your side when you hear how great your paintings are—from somebody besides me."

She felt like her face could break, her smile was so wide. Her evening just flipped from stressful to wonderful with his heartfelt words.

"Now I can't wait to mingle. Let's go!" She tugged at his hand. "I want to visit every suite and hear their comments firsthand. Even if some are a bit critical, I can take it."

And she knew she could. Everyone didn't need to love her work. That would be impossible, not even desirable. The fact that she was recognized as someone to watch out for in the artistic circles was more than enough for now.

An exhilarating and exhausting hour later, Trey strode onto the Trillium Terrace cocktail reception and scanned the bustling crowd for Delaney. There she was! Her dark, shiny hair swung easily across her bare shoulders as she spoke to Rob Unger, a youngish Weatherall executive from the London office. Her hands flew as she talked, and he wondered if she was describing a scene somewhere, waiting to be painted. Rob's inane smile and attentive body language indicated he was completely entranced by the gorgeous artist.

Blowing out a long breath, Trey strode across the terrace, beelining for the chatting couple. *Stay cool,* he chided himself. *After all, she's a free agent.*

He stuck his hand out to shake Rob's hand. "Glad to see you could make it." *Now, you've seen the place, why don't you take your James Bond accent and take a hike back to London*. "I hope you can stay a few days. Try your hand at fishing, maybe?"

"Can't Trey. But thanks. You know how it is. I'm catching a connecting flight from your little airport in"—he checked his Rolex—"about thirty minutes."

"That's too bad." *Good to know*. "Maybe next time."

Delaney politely nodded and slipped into the crowd, leaving the two men alone. Rob leaned in slightly, "From what I hear, you won't be here much longer either. Can't say any more, but you're one lucky devil, Trey."

Ignoring the reference to his likely promotion, Trey forced a smile and stuck his hand out for the second time. "Good flight, Rob. See you at the AGM."

Like a black cloud rolling over the summer sun, Trey's mood descended to melancholy as he considered Rob's prediction. He'd always known his tenure here at the Loon Lake Nirvana was short-lived, but he didn't want to go. He'd miss a lot of things about Loon Lake and the friendly little village. This was new, he noted, slightly uncomfortable with the emotion.

He glanced over at Delaney. Now she was in the center of a group of artsy reporter types, all attentively recording her remarks. Tomorrow's papers would be full of her quotes, he knew.

Happiness radiated off her face. She was having the time of her life. And he was glad for her. Confidence only made her more beautiful. In Paris, she would grow even more as an artist. Finally get the acclaim she deserved after five years in artistic exile—Buttermilk Falls style.

She lifted her head for a moment and her shining, cat's-eye green eyes caught his. His feet stopped moving and a cold band of steel tightened around his chest—and the truth slammed him hard.

He couldn't tell Delaney that he'd fallen in love with her. Not now. She needed and deserved Paris. His stomach clenched. He could lose her forever if she went, he knew.

Lifting her hand, she waved her slender fingers in acknowledgment and blew him a kiss. *All very Parisian,* he thought, returning her smile.

Chapter Nineteen

Roland Weatherall Sr. was a bulky, imposing man on any given day. Put him in a double-breasted black tux and up on a podium, his looming silhouette clearly commandeered attention. Just as he raised his champagne glass and called for everyone's attention, the automatic dusk-to-dawn patio lights flickered on.

"I'm delighted to be here on this perfect summer night to once again thank everyone for attending the Nirvana Hotel's gala. I'm extremely proud of the efforts of our Loon Lake team on creating a one-of-a-kind penthouse floor.

"As many of you know, the rest of the hotel has been open for several months. My son, Ethan Weatherall, created the one-of-a-kind glass-topped lobby and the amazing Starlight Room. He has already received accolades for his flagship hotel's design excellence in the industry's journals."

A soft patter of applause rippled across the rose-scented terrace.

"Tonight we celebrate the interim manager of the Loon Lake's Nirvana, Trey Sullivan."

He motioned for Trey to join him on the podium. "Trey has topped off the Nirvana with his own forward-thinking vision." More applause.

Goose bumps shot up Delaney's arms and they had nothing to do with the cooling evening air. Mr. Weatherall's obvious pride and confidence in Trey warmed her heart. She stood taller with his continuing words of praise, happily sharing in Trey's glory.

"And at this time I would ask the man responsible for originally conceptualizing this hotel, Ethan Weatherall, to join us on the stage."

Delaney squealed and turned, following the attentive crowd's lead, to face the lobby door. If Ethan had returned for this surprise visit, then Lily must be there too!

Ethan, looking tanned and fit, appeared from within the crowd and strode to the podium.

Delaney was struck with how relaxed and happy Ethan looked. His extended honeymoon obviously had agreed with him. *Apparently that's what love will do for you,* she concluded, recalling the uptight, stressed-out Ethan she'd met a year ago.

But where was Lily? Her friend was reserved, tending to avoid the spotlight—except of course, when fighting against an environmental affront. Then, she was the first up on the soapbox.

Delaney stood on her tiptoes and scanned the sea of heads. There she was! Her best friend stood at the edge of the crowd, her shoulder-length blond locks caught up in an elegant chignon. Long, drop pearl earrings dangled against her golden skin. A big change from the wind-tousled, sweatshirt-wearing marine biologist Delaney knew and loved. She waved her over.

"Lily! I'm so glad to see you!" Relief flowed through her as she flung her arms around Lily's slender form. Finally, someone who could give her some sensible advice. She'd never appreciated her best friend more than now. "You rat! Why didn't you tell me you were flying home?"

"I'm sorry, but Ethan wanted to surprise Trey," she said, returning her friend's hug. "And it was all a bit last minute. Plus I knew you and Trey were going nuts here the last few days, and I didn't want to bother you."

They linked arms and turned their attention back to their men on the podium.

Ethan spoke first. "I can't thank Trey enough for stepping up and propelling this hotel to the next level while I was vacationing with my new wife." Heads turned. Lily ducked hers in embarrassment. "I intend to continue to execute my duties as CEO of the Canadian Nirvana chain of hotels from right here on Loon Lake. My wife and I have already begun to build our home."

This was not news to Delaney, but she hugged Lily again, unable to contain her delight.

"The new, long-term manager will arrive at Loon Lake tomorrow to pick up the reins."

Menacing clouds rolled over the twinkling stars, and the wind gusted from the north. Jason and the patio staff hustled to gather up the scattering napkins and such.

Ethan was saying something else about the impending arrival of new staff, but Delaney had tuned out.

Trey would leave, maybe tomorrow, for some exotic locale—Morocco, according to the hotel's rumor mill. It was all happening too fast. She wanted to run. Hide in her suite.

But she remained rooted to the floor, searching for a positive somewhere in this awful announcement. Maybe they might occasionally plan to meet while she was in France? She cheered a bit. *But no*, she admonished herself. *No, I won't be that girl—the pathetic one that chases around after a man after he's clearly moved on.*

"I'm pleased to announce that due to the incredible response to this hotel, senior management has decided to bring the Nirvana chain to . . ." Ethan paused for effect. "Asia."

The crowd shuffled and waited for his next words. "With Trey Sullivan helming the ship. He'll be overseeing all five Asian locations—from the ground up. Please welcome the new CEO of the Asian Nirvana chain of hotels." Ethan stepped back and Trey was urged to center stage.

A low rumble of enthusiasm swept the terrace,

followed by the rapid tapping of information into PDAs and laptops. Asia?

Delaney could hardly breathe. She knew he'd be offered something soon. He was Weatherall's valued go-to man. But this was huge. And exactly the kind of promotion Trey had been working toward.

She looked to Trey's face, trying to gauge his reaction. Obviously, the announcement had taken him off guard. Surprise, excitement, pride, and a millisecond of something she couldn't quite identify, all crossed his face. Quickly composing his face, Trey reached to shake both Ethan's and Mr. Weatherall's hand.

"Thank you for offering me this amazing opportunity," Trey said, directing his words to the ring of blue-suited executives surrounding him onstage. "Your confidence in me is appreciated. I'm confident Ethan's New Age vision of what a hotel needs to be in the twenty-first century will be welcomed in Asia, just as it has been here."

Delaney's limbs felt like lead. Her arm slipped from Lily's back. Trey looked so excited, in his element.

Suddenly she remembered how, just a few days ago, she'd almost confessed her true feelings. Thank goodness they'd been interrupted before she'd embarrassed herself—and him.

He smiled at the milling crowd. "But I can't take all the credit for the success of the penthouse. I couldn't have accomplished this without the unfaltering eye and creative genius of Delaney Forbes." Applause interrupted his speech. "Also, I know many of you were intrigued by the small oil paintings in each suite. For those of you who don't already know, the artist is none other than Delaney Forbes."

Applause rumbled all around her, and she managed a smile and gave an acknowledging wave.

"Come join me in the Starlight Room," he urged the onlookers. "We have so much to celebrate tonight."

The double doors to the Starlight Room swung open as if by magic, and in seconds the terrace emptied.

Delaney sank into a chair, relieved to be alone with her thoughts for a few minutes. Now she knew the true meaning of the term "emotional roller coaster."

Her feelings had run the gamut from fear and apprehension to elation and pride to confusion and sadness—all in the space of six hours. Exhaustion crept into her bones, molding her backbone into the upholstered chair back. She let her head drop back. The wind had cleaned the sky clear of clouds and the stars had returned. The same stars that hung over Asia. And Paris.

Loneliness engulfed her. Life without Trey?

Trying to focus on the positive, she reminded herself of the prestigious art reviewer she'd met earlier who had applauded her upcoming move to France. He'd even supplied her with names of galleries and dealers to see when she arrived. She glanced down at the card and the quickly scribbled Parisian addresses.

She sighed audibly. Timing is everything, they say. A month ago she would have been delirious with happiness. Tonight, her elation was tampered by an aching sadness.

A whiff of sandalwood, spicy and exotically Asian, drifted from the Starlight Room. A sultry jazz tune slowed the vibrant hum of voices from within, and she knew the couples had returned to their partners for the slow, sexy dance. Content to rest against one another and leave the talk for later, they'd cling and sway in the heat-charged room. Music tended to reach into a soul and bring to the top what was really important.

"Delaney."

It was Trey. He stood next to the table with two champagne glasses in his hand. "Hi," she said, turning her upturned head toward his voice. His tux still looked impeccable, but now there were tiny lines etched into the corner of his eyes and a faint shadow of a beard dulled his jawline.

"I was just about to come in. Just taking a minute to catch my breath. It's been a big day."

"You've got that right." Trey handed her one of the long-stemmed glasses. "It looks like both of us got what we were after." He raised his glass. "Congratulations on your rave reviews."

Not really a drinker, she felt the occasion deserved a marking of some sort. Accepting the glass, she took a tiny sip of the bubbling wine, resisting the urge to wrinkle her nose when the desert-dry liquid hit the back of her throat. She pressed a fingertip to the end of her nose and blinked her eyes. People actually liked this stuff?

"Thanks," she said, choosing to ignore his sideways grin. "And to you too." She raised the glass. "Asia, no less. That's amazing. Even you won't get bored with a big project like that. Five hotels! You'll be popping from city to city every week, I imagine."

His stepped in closer. The sweet smell of his musky aftershave still lingering on his skin at this late hour, lured her into his space. Could she resist, if he opened his arms to her?

She twirled the stem of the crystal glass, and pressed its cool edge to her suddenly over-warm cheek.

"And you," Trey said. "You'll be right where you belong. Living in the heart of the Parisian art district, all paint-spattered and smelling of turpentine."

His hand stretched forward, and he gently tucked a strand of her wind-mussed hair behind her ear. In her hurry to get ready this morning, had she missed a streak of paint again? she wondered.

His eyes twinkled like Loon Lake stars, his worry lines fading, as he continued to talk. "And you'll be all cute and sexy in those overalls you wear while you're working."

"Cute and sexy?" He must have drunk a couple of glasses of champagne already. "Okay. Stop right there. You're obviously delirious, or drunk. Or your newfound power must have temporarily short-circuited your brain." She poked him playfully in the ribs. "But I'll let it slide for tonight."

Placing his champagne glass on the table, he caught

her hand and pressed it to his chest, pulling her a step closer. "That was my first drink tonight. Not a great idea to overindulge at a function like this. I'm still running the hotel, officially, until tomorrow." He leaned in closer. "By the way, I love you in those crazy overalls."

"Well, you've always been a strange one," she joked. Or was he? After all, she'd considered him perfectly adorable when she'd run down to his office late in the afternoon and caught him with his shirtsleeves rolled up above his elbow, a fluorescent yellow highlighter stuck behind his ear, and a geeky pair of reading glasses stuck halfway down his nose.

Back in familiar territory and a more comfortable footing, she relaxed.

"How about a dance?" He stepped back and extended his hand to her in a move stolen from an old Gene Kelly movie. "I believe this is where it all began, my dear. Remember our first dinner, here on the Terrace?" He pushed his shoulders back in a bad Superman imitation and deepened his voice. "You know, the night I heroically rescued you from Flo and the terrible twosome."

As if she could ever forget. It was also the night they'd pledged to leave a clear path for the other. And, not fall in love.

"Of course I remember," she said, fighting back a hysterical giggle. "You stepped all over my toes on the dance floor."

"Well, how about it, then? Shall we end our acquaintance where it began?"

"Why not?" She slid her hand into his and they walked into the Starlight Room, just as the band oozed into Eric Clapton's "Wonderful Tonight."

Melting into his chest felt like a homecoming. All the parts fit perfectly. No jostling or settling required. One hand rested contentedly against his broad shoulder, her fingertips enjoying the luxurious fabric of his tux. Trey held her other hand just the right way. Not so tight as to be overly in charge, but just enough pressure to make a girl want to follow.

Boy, did she want to follow this man. Timbuktu, Morocco, Asia.

She blinked hard. Her head drifted lower, her cheek now crushed against his lapel. Fainter, but just as irresistible, his designer aftershave further confused her senses. Not to mention her sensibilities.

There was no way she would ever pull out the commitment card on this guy now. His career was tied to a rocket, and eventually she'd become an anchor.

She straightened her posture, missed a step, and apologized. Not for any man would she sacrifice her dignity. She drudged up her old mantra: *Think Paris. Think Paris. Think Paris.*

"Delaney? That's the third time you've tromped on *my* toes." He stepped back and settled a fatherly style gaze on her face. "You're tired. Why don't we call it a night?"

"Sorry about the toes. I am tired." She glanced around the room. No sign of any of the Weatherall clan. "I guess there's no need for me to hang around any longer."

"By the way, Lily and Ethan slipped out a while ago—jet-lagged. Or at least that's their story," he said with a smile. "Lily said she'd call you in the morning."

Together, they walked toward the elevator, as they had so many times before. He punched Penthouse and the door opened almost immediately. They stepped in and the door swished closed.

They stood side by side, the six inches between them feeling like a mile. She knew this was the end of everything. Their work together. Everything.

In a tone that she'd only heard him use in a business meeting, he said, "It's been a profound pleasure to work with you, Delaney. I hope, if nothing else, this job has rebooted your confidence in your talent. Go to Paris and knock 'em dead."

Her throat thickened, and she concentrated on breathing normally. Focusing on the crack between the doors, she silently repeated her mantra again.

"I'll be in meetings all day tomorrow—with the Weatherall executives—finalizing the details. So," he glanced in her direction, "I'll say good-bye tonight."

"Sure," she croaked out, before coughing into her cupped hand. Was this really it then? "I'll be busy packing up tomorrow anyway. You know . . . Paris and everything."

The doors breezed open and they exited the elevator, and he politely gestured to her to go ahead. Always gallant, if nothing else.

Her four-inch heels that she'd made a special trip

back to 31 Lilac Lane for, clacked against the tile as she hurried along the stunning corridor she'd help create.

Her door was first, and she already had the key card poised for action. She stuck it in the slot. *He better not try to kiss me tonight, or I'll loose it completely.* At this point she wasn't sure if it was love or disappointment that had her so upset.

Apparently he wasn't nearly as conflicted, since he only paused briefly at her door.

"Good night, Delaney. And thanks again. Without you, I'd never have accomplished all this," he said, waving in the direction of the gleaming driftwood sculpture.

He flashed a glance to her face, but quickly dropped his gaze. Like most men with commitment phobias, he was probably squeamish when confronted with real emotion, she decided, in a desperate but unsuccessful attempt to excuse his behavior.

"Keep in touch."

His words sounded like something off a Hallmark card. Polite, friendly. Generic.

She pushed hard against her door. Darkness enveloped her as she stepped across the threshold. The metallic click of the door incised the silent space, punctuating the end of all things Trey. She stretched her hand to the wall to collect her bearings. She threw her purse to the corner and almost made it to the bed before the sobs, rising from her belly, shook her body.

Chapter Twenty

The next morning the sun dawned only to fight its way though a thick layer of billowing gray clouds. *Perfect,* Delaney considered as she dragged open the floor-to-ceiling drapes. *The weather is totally in sync with my life.*

Bleary-eyed from her sleepless night, she glanced at her watch: 6:45 A.M. If she hustled, she might make it out of the building before Trey came down for breakfast. The last thing she wanted was an awkward elevator ride with Trey. Checking her watch again, she hurried to the bathroom.

Nineteen minutes later, showered, dressed, and packed, she pressed zero on her phone and requested help with her bags.

Soon Jason was at her door, a large luggage trolley positioned at his side. "Good morning, Miss Forbes. Sorry to see you leave. I hope your stay here was enjoyable."

She nodded in response to the young man's polite inquiry. "It was, Jason. Thanks." It wasn't a lie. For the most part it'd been fabulous. Living the high life, dining and dancing, room service at her fingertips. Exactly what she'd imagined when she signed on for the job. And what a job! Her paintings now hung on the walls of a five-star hotel, with rave reviews to boot.

"Yes, it has been amazing, in so many ways." All Trey had done was keep up his end of their bargain. No reason to resent him for that. She raised her chin and forced a smile. *Paris, here I come. Much stronger for my time spent here, thanks to Trey.*

Thankfully, the elevator was empty of other guests. As much as she wanted to connect with Lily, she'd wait until she was at home again. Right now it was paramount she leave the hotel and her broken heart behind.

Flo had phoned a few days before to tell her that her house was smoke-free and ready for occupation again, the tenants not moving in until next week.

Thanks again to Jason, a car waited for her in the circular drive. She was whisked down the drive, through the dusty, tree-lined mile that led to the village's familiar streets.

The small, white house never looked so good, she thought as the car crunched its way up her graveled driveway. She popped open the door handle, and the driver scurried to retrieve her luggage.

Standing at the bottom of the steps, she studied the white-clad, two-story building. Gingerbread trim rimmed the roof. The tidy picket fence running along the property's perimeter was laden with blooming clematis vine. She drew in the sweet flavor of home and smiled her first genuine smile of the day. *It's beautiful.*

She couldn't wait to sleep in her own bed. Peek through the kitchen's crisp, polka-dotted café curtains at her shaggy backyard grass.

Maybe pop down to the Bluebird and nose out what she'd missed in Buttermilk Falls proper, while she'd been living a fairy-tale life at the Nirvana.

Two steps in, the kitchen's wall phone jangled, its ring jarring, after becoming accustomed to the muted tones of her hotel's state-of-the-art system.

She dropped her keys on the counter and hurried across the checkerboard linoleum, her heart fluttering in her chest. Maybe it was Trey?

"Hey, girlfriend."

It was Lily. "Hi, there. I thought honeymooners slept till noon."

Lily giggled and relayed Delaney's words to Ethan, a mildly annoying habit, Delaney noted, of which cohabiting lovebirds overly indulged.

"Well, we're not officially on our honeymoon anymore," Lily replied. "Home to stay. Ethan checked with the contractors this morning. Our house should be ready in about eight weeks."

"That's great news. Have you told Emma yet?"

"Phoned her an hour ago. Emma is thrilled about moving to Loon Lake. She loved her stay with Mom and Dad at the Hideaway and she talked nonstop about the deer that feed just outside the kitchen window. And because she enjoyed Emma's company so much, Mom has decided to start volunteering at Tay Valley's Down's Syndrome Day-Away Center!"

"That's wonderful, Lily."

"Ethan and I are heading over to surprise Emma now. And guess what!"

Lily didn't wait for a reply, but Delaney didn't mind a bit. She'd missed her friend's chatter. E-mails just weren't nearly as much fun.

"The three of us are staying in your gorgeous penthouse suites until the house is done!"

So now it was Lily's turn to experience eight weeks of the suite life. "Perfect. Let me know your impressions, after you've been there for a while. I'd be interested."

"Of course," Lily said, her voice lowering to a subdued tone. "I can't believe you're leaving, just when I get back home."

"I know, our timing is the pits." She dragged a red and black chrome chair from the kitchen table and plunked down, feeling as if her guiding stars were a tad out of alignment at the moment. "But you know how long I've waited for my year in Paris."

"I know. But, I thought maybe. . . . things might have. . . . changed. Maybe?"

What was her intuitive friend hinting at? That was

the thing about best friends, they dug until they unearthed all your secrets. Had she zeroed in on the attraction between her and Trey in one short evening?

"No. Nothing's changed." *Well, actually everything has changed.* "Flo is sending over my tenant's post-dated rent checks later today, and I'm hopping a plane for Paris day after tomorrow."

In the wee hours last night, Delaney had decided against pouring out her heart to Lily. Sweet, softhearted Lily would feel impelled to persuade Trey to commit to poor, lovestruck Delaney. And that was something she couldn't risk. Especially after Trey's casual send-off last night.

"Then let's have lunch at the Bluebird today," Lily tossed out, apparently willing to abandon the other more intriguing thread of conversation for now.

Delaney's spirits rose. Now that's just what she needed. Lunch with Lily. "Let's. See you at noon, okay? I'll try to snag our table."

She replaced the receiver, grabbed the smaller of the suitcases still stacked by the back door, and padded up the stairs to her childhood bedroom.

She only needed to throw Lily off the scent for one day, and her secret would go with her, unspoken, to Paris.

Thankfully, in an airport this small, lineups almost never happened, Delaney observed.

During construction of the Nirvana, a deal had been struck with the municipality. Weatherall provided the property and financed the construction of the airstrip, leaving the administrative costs of the operation to the council. A real coup for both parties.

"Your plane's still being fueled up, Delaney," Ted Sherman called out. "May as well grab a coffee while you wait."

Delaney eyed the hulking coffee machine centered between the chips and chocolate bar dispensers. "Thanks, Ted, I think I'll just read a magazine. Just let me know when the plane's ready, please."

Selecting a tattered magazine from the rack, she eyed the empty waiting room with satisfaction. She'd invited Lily and Ethan over for a barbecue last evening and they'd said their good-byes.

Propping her feet on her carry-on, she wiggled against the molded plastic of her chair and opened her magazine. Flipping carelessly through the glossy ads, she congratulated herself for managing to make her escape from Buttermilk Falls with minimum fanfare. Thank heavens her parents were in Calgary, or there would have been a cake and streamers.

The last thing she wanted was a tearful, emotional good-bye. As it was, she was just barely holding it together. Tears lay just beneath the surface, and she'd likely come undone, if pressed.

During their lunch at the Bluebird, Lily had peppered her with pointed questions about Delaney's suite life at the Nirvana. Had she ever ordered chocolate cake at midnight? What had it been like working with

Trey? Did swimming in the indoor pool dry out her hair? Didn't she love Trey's sense of humor?

Delaney easily countered with her own line of questioning. Does it really rain in England all the time? Would they return to the Mediterranean for their fifth anniversary, as Lily had sworn in a passionate e-mail sent from Italy?

Only when she told Lily how she came to paint again did Delaney stop censoring her words. She detailed the progression of her artistic renaissance, including Trey's supportive role. She didn't even care that the Gadabout Girls had put down their forks and had shushed the chattering children twirling aimlessly atop the café's vinyl-topped barstools in order to hear the conversation better.

"Delaney." A deep, masculine voice returned her to real time.

Her breath caught in her throat. The magazine slipped from her hands. Trey stood beside her suitcases, his hands stuffed into his jeans' pockets.

She remained seated, her body cemented to the chair. What was going on? Had something happened to Lily? She looked past Trey through the glass to the parking lot and Trey's unoccupied car.

"What are you doing here?" She knew her tone bordered on rude, but her plane was now rolling toward the terminal.

Under his tan, he looked pale. He shifted uneasily from one foot to another and cast a glance toward the approaching plane. "Look. I know my timing is bad, but I really need to tell you something."

"Okay, go ahead." Hope fluttered her chest. *No. It can't possibly be.*

A plane buzzed the terminal like a big, annoying bee and she shifted ahead on her seat to better hear his words. He grabbed her hands and pulled her to a standing position. Their noses practically touching, his breath fanned her cheek.

He spoke rapidly, as if he didn't say his piece quickly, he'd lose his nerve. "I love you. I know I said I wouldn't fall for you, but I did. You, this place, changed me. I want to be with you. That is, when you're ready. After Paris, of course." His grip tightened on her hands. His chest rose and fell under his shirt as he watched her with boy-like expectancy.

Her knees like water, she lifted her hand and touched his face with her open palm. "Oh, Trey." He wasn't asking her to give up Paris. He was willing to wait while she lived her dream.

The tears that had been threatening for three days clouded her eyes. He loved her. The big old black-and-white movie way.

"I don't want Paris anymore," she confessed. "I stopped needing Paris when I started painting again. I want to stay here. Paint where I love and understand the landscape. I was only still going to Paris to try and get over you."

He tipped her chin with his fingertip and looked at

her, naked vulnerability replacing his usual confidence. "So what are you saying?"

She flung her arms around his neck. "I'm saying that I love you too. That I wanted to end our stupid pact weeks ago."

Her words were barely out and he was kissing her. Her lips, her cheeks, her chin, her forehead.

She pulled back in his arms and looked into his face, anxious to sort through the complications of a long-distance relationship. "Hey, maybe after Asia, Weatherall will bring you back to work on this continent," she said, trying to inject optimism in her voice.

"I turned it down."

"You what!" Stunned, she gulped hard. "I don't understand."

"I'm done with living out of a suitcase. I want a real life."

And he wants it with me. Pure joy coursed through her veins. Out of the corner of her eye, she saw Ted covertly watching them, a smile tugging at the corner of his mouth.

"I know of at least three deserving Weatherall executives primed and waiting for an opportunity like Asia," Trey continued. He steadied his gaze and looked directly into her eyes. "I asked Mr. Weatherall for the job of permanent manager, here at Loon Lake."

What? He'd passed on the Asian project before he knew she no longer wanted to go to Paris. The last of her doubts fell away.

"I can't think of a better place to live, once we're married," he ventured, "than 31 Lilac Lane, Buttermilk Falls, Ontario."

She snuggled into his arms, thrilled at the thought of raising a family in her childhood home. "Just one little problem, Trey. My tenants are moving in day after tomorrow. I deposited their rent checks in the bank yesterday."

"Hey, you're forgetting that I'm the go-to guy. There are no problems, only solutions. How about we give them a complimentary penthouse suite—for whatever time they need to find another house."

She melted back into his waiting arms. "I knew there was a reason I fell for you."